Sharon,

Thank you for the support & reviews!

xo

Rebecca

Take the Storm

Also From Rebecca Zanetti

Scorpius Syndrome
Scorpius Rising (On the Hunt anthology)
Mercury Striking

Dark Protectors
Fated
Claimed
Tempted
Hunted
Consumed
Provoked
Twisted
Shadowed
Tamed
Marked
Wicked Ride (Realm Enforcers)
Wicked Edge (Realm Enforcers)

Sin Brothers series
Forgotten Sins
Sweet Revenge
Blind Faith
Total Surrender

Maverick Montana Cowboys
Against the Wall
Under the Covers
Rising Assets
Over the Top

Take the Storm
By Rebecca Zanetti

Rising Storm
Episode 6

Story created by Julie Kenner and Dee Davis

EVIL EYE
CONCEPTS

Take the Storm, Episode 6
Rising Storm
Copyright 2015 Julie Kenner and Dee Davis Oberwetter
ISBN: 978-1-942299-19-6

Published by Evil Eye Concepts, Incorporated

All rights reserved. No part of this book may be reproduced, scanned, or distributed in any printed or electronic form without permission. Please do not participate in or encourage piracy of copyrighted materials in violation of the author's rights.

This is a work of fiction. Names, places, characters, and incidents are the product of the author's imagination and are fictitious. Any resemblance to actual persons, living or dead, events or establishments is solely coincidental.

Acknowledgments from the Author

This project has been so much fun, and I have a couple of folks to thank. First, thank you to Julie Kenner for calling me up and saying… "So. Have you ever wanted to take part in a soap opera?" I'm honored to be included with this group!

Thanks to Dee Davis as well as Julie for creating this wild world in Storm, Texas.

A big thank you goes to Elizabeth Berry of 1001 Dark Nights for including me in her whirlwind of a world and for being my friend, in addition to all the hard work and brilliant ideas that she generously shares.

Thanks to MJ Rose of Evil Eye Concepts for the hard work and genius promotional plans.

As always, thank you to Big Tone, Gabe, and Karly for the patience and fun times…you're the best!

Foreword

Dear reader –

We have wanted to do a project together for over a decade, but nothing really jelled until we started to toy with a kernel of an idea that sprouted way back in 2012 … and ultimately grew into Rising Storm.

We are both excited about and proud of this project—not only of the story itself, but also the incredible authors who have helped bring the world and characters we created to life.

We hope you enjoy visiting Storm, Texas. Settle in and stay a while!

Happy reading!

Julie Kenner & Dee Davis

Sign up for the Rising Storm/1001 Dark Nights Newsletter and be entered to win an exclusive lightning bolt necklace specially designed for Rising Storm by Janet Cadsawan of Cadsawan.com.

Go to http://risingstormbooks.com/necklace to subscribe.

As a bonus, all subscribers will receive a free
Rising Storm story
Storm Season: Ginny & Jacob – the Prequel
by Dee Davis

CHAPTER 1

Stars glittered across the wide Texas sky, reflecting off the dark lake. No wind disturbed the calm surface, which was good, because some idiot had piled the bonfire too high. Flames crackled into the night, their sound competing with laughter and teenage murmurs. School was over, summer was here, and it was time for freedom and fun. For most kids.

Luis Moreno sat on a piece of driftwood, facing the fire, his arms dangling between his knees. The stitches in his left hand itched, and a hollow ache in his chest hurt.

His life sucked.

Mallory Alvarez, the girl he'd love until he fucking died, laughed easily with a bunch of guys from the football team. She looked tiny next to the guys, and her dark jeans curved over an amazing ass. They stood on the beach, closer to the shore, and every once in a while the stud quarterback would pretend he was going to throw her in.

She'd giggle and move to the other side of the small huddle.

Luis knew that laugh—it was fun and full of friendship. Even so, jealousy crawled up his torso and clogged his throat. He was now firmly in the *friend zone*, too. Because of one stupid, really stupid, mistake.

The *mistake* lounged over on a picnic blanket on the other side of the fire, wearing way too short shorts and a white see-through blouse with a purple bra underneath. Lacey Salt. A week ago, he would've been totally obsessing about that bra.

Now, after she'd tried to seduce him and he'd rejected her, he was left alone wishing Mallory would take him back. At least she'd forgiven him, saying she didn't want to lose him as a friend.

Being her friend wasn't enough. He wasn't sure he was even friends with Lacey any longer, either.

She leaned against Freddy Phillips, who was a senior and definitely a player. He was obviously trying to get into her pants, most likely because she now had a reputation of being easy.

"Dude. Stop pouting." Jeffry Rush, his best friend, shoved a red cup into his hand and dropped next to him on the driftwood, holding his own cup.

Luis frowned and sniffed the drink, drawing back when his nostrils burned. "What the heck?"

"Moonshine." Jeffry stared into his own cup. "The genuine article from Cooder. A couple of the seniors stole it from some dive bar outside of town." Cooder was almost famous in the small town of Storm, having brewed and sold moonshine for decades without the law ever catching up to him.

"You don't drink," Luis said slowly.

Jeffry shrugged. "Who'd care?"

Luis took a deep breath. He'd never tried moonshine and wasn't sure it was a great idea. "If we're gonna drink, we should probably stick with beer, you know?"

Jeffry took a sip and grimaced. His shoulders slumped, and even his sigh sounded bummed. "We don't have beer."

"Um, I'm the first to admit that I don't understand political crap, but if your dad is running for reelection, you getting caught with Cooder's moonshine is a seriously bad idea." Luis had been so busy with his own problems, he'd once again forgotten his friend didn't have the best life once you really looked inside it. His dad was a state senator, and they always had to keep up appearances, whatever the hell that meant. "Empty your cup and I'll do the same."

"No. I'm tired of elections and of having to smile all the damn time. Tired of pretending I'm happy and stuck being a certain way." Jeffry tipped back a drink and sputtered, coughing until Luis smacked him on the back. "This is terrible."

Luis grinned. "It's probably not supposed to taste good."

Lacey squealed across the fire and sat up, coughing as well.

Shit. Now Lacey was drinking that stuff? Luis quickly glanced over to make sure Mallory wasn't putting that crap in her body. She'd be sick in minutes, and the stuff was so strong, it could actually cause damage. Her hands were in her pockets, and she was still talking to the quarterback.

Did she like him?

Luis sighed. What the heck. He took a deep drink of the moonshine. The liquid burned down his throat and exploded in his gut. His legs trembled. "Holy crap." Sucking in air, he pressed a hand to his abdomen. "We might as well drink gasoline," he gasped. Almost instantly, his head started to swim.

Mallory was staring at him, disbelief wrinkling her nose. Then disappointment.

Damn it. She'd seen him drink. He coughed again, surprised when flames didn't exhale with his breath. Now besides being a two-timing loser, he was breaking the law and drinking rotgut when he should be trying to win her back. Maybe he should've had sex with her when she wanted to do it, but he respected her and thought they should wait.

If they hadn't waited, then they'd probably be together right now, snuggling and watching the fire.

Jeffry threw him a shoulder. Even at the lake, he wore a pressed golf shirt and perfectly creased beige shorts, his hair unruffled. "If you're so sad, go talk to her. Mallory is the best. She'll forgive you."

"She has." Luis tugged on his faded Jack Daniels T-shirt he'd tossed on with his regular swim trunks. Maybe he should make more of an effort with clothes like Jeffry did. Would Mallory roll her eyes or be impressed? Knowing Mal, she'd just laugh. Would they ever get back together? He sniffed the drink again and licked his lips. Now a nice warmth spread throughout him. "Mallory only wants to be friends."

Jeffry rolled his eyes. "She wants to be more than friends, but you hurt her. You have to suck up for a while, man."

"Yeah?" Luis studied his friend, trying to focus. Jeffry was the smartest person Luis had ever met, and he had a knack for understanding people. Well, people other than his own family. "You think I could get her back?"

"Definitely." Jeffry smiled, his grin a little lopsided. "But you're gonna have to grovel, and you have to stay away from crazy Lacey."

Now that wasn't exactly fair. "Lacey is not crazy. Her brother died, her family is acting weird, and she's lost." Of course, a lost Lacey was a battering ram of destructiveness. "Is she still letting people think we slept together?"

"Yep."

It's like she wanted people gossiping about her, even if the talk was bad. Lacey and Mallory had been best friends forever, and it was like Lacey didn't care about that. Or her reputation. Or Luis's friendship. They hadn't had sex because he'd stopped them.

He cleared his throat. "I thought that maybe you and Lacey—"

"God no." Jeffry leaned back, horror filling his eyes right before red filled his face. "Definitely no. Not for me."

Geez. She wasn't that bad. "Okay. Sorry." Why didn't Jeffry seem interested in any of the local girls? More than one of them had asked him out, and he always turned them down. "I just thought you and Lacey could be close," Luis mumbled.

She caught him watching her, and she stood, swaying just a little.

He tensed, just in case she fell toward the fire. Instead, she regained her footing and kicked off her flip-flops. Tossing her brown hair over a shoulder, she walked barefoot in the sand and around the fire. Her butt swayed, and her gaze stayed hot on him.

"Ruh roe," Jeffry slurred into his cup, turning his gaze to the sand.

Luis tensed. He could actually feel Mallory's eyes on him. Maybe Lacey would keep going. Perhaps she needed to take a squat somewhere. He looked down to check out Jeffry's leather loafers. The things probably cost more than he made in a month.

Bright pink toenails stopped in his view.

He sighed and looked up toned legs, past the purple bra, to Lacey's flushed face. "I hope you're not driving," he muttered, his voice sounding a little weird. The moonshine had actually scratched his throat.

She reached out and ruffled his hair. "Is that an offer?"

Her touch did nothing but make him cringe. She was messing with him, and she was trying to hurt Mallory for some reason. Temper slid through him, and he fought to remain in control. "Stop it, Lacey."

"*Stop it, Lacey,*" she mimicked, lowering her voice. "That's all you say now."

He stood just so she'd have to stop playing with his hair. The world tilted for a moment, and he sucked down some air to regain his balance.

When everything righted, he focused on her. "Why are you telling lies about me?"

She blinked. "I haven't lied."

"You haven't told anybody the truth," he spat out, heat climbing up his face. "Everyone is acting like I'm some manwhore hero, and they're calling you a slut. Why do you want that?"

Her pretty face lost color, leaving her lips white. "At least they're noticing me."

"That is so fucked up," he muttered, the fight leaving him. His temples started to pound. Why couldn't things just go back to the way they were only a couple of weeks ago? "I know you're hurting, but this isn't helping."

Mallory suddenly appeared at his elbow. "We need to talk, Luis."

His mouth dropped open.

Lacey turned a big-toothed smile on Mallory. "Sorry, but I'm not done with Luis." She ran a hand down his arm like she had every right to touch him.

Jeffry sighed and shoved to his feet. "Everybody stop acting so weird. Let's all go back to normal, okay?"

"Oh, hell no." Mallory put her hands on her hips. "We can't go back, because Lacey is a desperate, two-faced, pathetic wannabe slut. It's too bad you can't find anybody to sleep with, and I know Luis rejected you."

Luis blinked. He'd never heard Mallory talk in a voice like that. "Um—"

Lacey rounded on Mallory. "You're just pissed he turned you down and then wanted me."

Mallory gasped.

"I didn't tell her—" Luis started and then winced.

Triumph lit up Lacey's features. "I knew it."

Mallory turned to spin away, and Luis grabbed her arm to pull her back. "Listen. I wanted to wait because I care about you and want it to be perfect. No other reason." Yeah, she'd wanted to have sex, maybe, and he'd put the brakes on. Not because of Lacey, but because he wasn't ready. Or he hadn't thought he was ready.

Lacey laughed. "If a guy really loves you, he doesn't say no."

Mallory's jaw trembled and then firmed.

That was it. Maybe it was the booze, maybe it was the hurt, but Luis lost it. He threw out his arms and started to yell. "Lacey, stop telling people we slept together. We did not, because I said no." Everyone went silent around them and turned to watch. He angled toward Mallory. "Mal, I love you. You want to have sex, I'm there. Name the time, name the place...hell. Name the position, and I am there with a condom."

He caught movement from the corner of his eye, but Lacey's fist plowed into his cheek before he could fully turn. His head jerked back and pain flared beneath his eye.

"You bitch!" Mallory leaped in front of him, both hands striking into Lacey's hair.

Lacey hissed and slapped Mallory in the face.

"Girl fight!" a guy yelled from near the beach.

The girls shrieked and grappled, rage in the sounds. Luis grabbed for Mallory while Jeffry tried to wade in and stop Lacey's flailing arms. She raked her nails down his wrist, and he yelped.

Luis stepped to the side, slid an arm around Mal's waist, and pivoted, putting her directly behind him. Her nails scratched his bicep in the movement. His heart thundered, and his breath panted out. He'd never used his size against anybody, and he really didn't like it.

Jeffry had both arms wrapped around Lacey from behind, and she was struggling furiously, her feet kicking sand.

"Stop." Luis tried to put command into his voice.

She fought harder, and Jeffry finally shook her. "Stop it, Lacey," he murmured in her ear. "Fight's over." He held tight until she finally gave up. Tears filled her eyes.

"Take her home," Luis said wearily.

Jeffry nodded and spun Lacey, walking her toward the cars. She stumbled against him, but the fight had gone out of her.

Luis slowly turned around.

Tears poured down Mallory's face, and shock filled her eyes. "I'm just like my dad," she whispered.

The words were a punch to the gut. Mal's dad was a mean drunk who hit his wife. "No, you're not." Luis reached out and tried to wipe off her face, but her tears kept coming. "You don't get drunk, and you'd never hit anybody smaller than you."

"I shouldn't hit anybody ever," she said, her voice breaking.

He tried to tug her into him, but she pushed him away. "I have to go." She turned in the sand and all but ran up the embankment toward the cars.

His legs itched with the need to run after her, but he'd pushed her around enough for a lifetime. He couldn't ever remind her of her jerk of a father, and he never wanted to use his strength against her except to protect her. How had things become so mixed up? With a groan, he dropped back onto his seat as the party resumed around him. Almost absently, he picked up his half-full cup of White Lightning.

What the hell. He tipped back the drink and tried to fill the emptiness inside him.

CHAPTER 2

Brittany Rush leaned against her car in the parking lot of Murphy's Pub, her entire body going into overdrive the moment Marcus Alvarez parked his car across the lot. He stretched out, and the second his gaze landed on her, a masculine grin lifted his lips.

Lips that had been on hers not too long ago, making her feel things she'd never felt before with any other guy.

She crossed her arms and pushed from her vehicle.

He lost the smile. With a barely discernable tilt of his head, he headed for her, his long strides quickly eating up the distance. "Something up, princess?"

"Dick," she breathed before thinking.

His upper lip quirked. "Care to expand on that?"

Anger roared through her so quickly her head heated. "You. Are. A. Dick."

He lifted a shoulder, too much amusement in his dark eyes. "I've been called worse, but never by somebody so pretty."

Oh, his condescension was about to get him kicked in the balls. She shifted her weight.

He must've read something in her face, because he lost the attitude, his hands going up in placation. "Your text just said to meet you here, and I didn't even know something was wrong." Slowly, he reached out and pushed a wayward curl away from her cheek. "What did I do?"

Hurt exploded in her. "You failed to mention you were leaving and going back to Montana."

His breath caught, moving his chest. "Oh." He grimaced and ran a hand through his thick hair. "Yeah, I suck." He tucked both hands into his pockets, his eyes somehow darkening further. "I promised to go back before I got here, and before you and I, well, I mean…"

Her eyes actually stung, but she wouldn't cry in front of him. "Great."

He shook his head. "I hadn't expected you."

Oh. She wet her lips. What did that mean? "Whatever."

He reached out to set both hands on her hips. "Listen. I should've told you, and I'm sorry I didn't, but I've had so much fun with you that I didn't want to think about leaving."

His sincerity melted through her. "I get that." For now, she allowed his hands to remain on her. "But what does that mean for us?"

He studied her and then shrugged. "I really don't know, but I'd like to find out. See what we could be."

The words eased the pain inside her chest. Was there a chance he'd stay? If her life in politics had taught her anything, it was to never push an issue. Not one that mattered. "So we jump in with both feet?"

"Yeah." He pressed a kiss to her forehead before leaning back. "How about we keep exploring a little bit and see where we end up? Nothing is set in stone."

She smiled, hope unfurling. Maybe he'd stay in Texas. "That seems fair. You owe me a drink, I believe."

He pulled her into his side and turned them toward the pub. "At least one."

* * * *

Patrick Murphy kicked back in the booth, feeling as empty as the beer mug in front of him. At almost midnight, a nice and rather mellow crowd hung out in Murphy's Pub, most people somewhat coupled off. Not him. "I'm a lone wolf," he muttered, jumping when his mom slid another Guinness in front of him and kept on walking by to clear a table by the door.

The chatter of family and friends around him was as familiar as the smell of beer, oiled wood, and peanut dust. He was home.

He sipped the potent brew, his gaze lingering on the couples. His older brother, Dillon, helped out behind the bar on his night off from being sheriff. That way, from what Patrick could tell, Dillon could keep an eye on Joanne Alvarez, who sat quietly in the corner with a friend sipping a Cosmo. Dillon had recently run Joanne's husband, a guy who beat her mercilessly, out of town.

If they ever got together and she found out, she was gonna be pissed. Or, well, perhaps she wouldn't be so mad considering her gaze kept roaming right toward Dillon.

Patrick's younger brother, Logan, sat on a barstool next to the pregnant Ginny Moreno. The baby's father had died in a car crash earlier in the spring, and now Logan and Ginny were starting something up.

A chill skittered down Patrick's spine. There were rumors about whether or not she'd named the real father, but he wouldn't listen to rumors. He'd back his brother.

Next to Logan, his best friend, Marcus Alvarez, sipped a beer, kept an eye on his mom, and flirted outrageously with Brittany Rush. Marcus was from the wrong side of the tracks, and Brittany was pretty much town royalty, so hey, that wasn't going to go south or anything.

Patrick sat up straighter as his mom slid into the booth beside him. "Keeping watch?" she murmured, her gaze going to the bar.

He nodded. "Yep. Have you ever just sensed the calm before a storm?"

She sighed, her blue eyes clouding. "Yes."

"Well, I'd like to take the storm away from here, but I don't think it's going to give us much warning." He took another drink and let the potent brew warm his belly.

His aunt Alice slipped into the booth on his other side, a glass of Harp in her hand. "Is Patrick watching over the family?" she asked her sister, ducking her head to survey the entire bar. As the elementary school principal, she had a way of seeing everything and everyone.

"Yes." His mom patted his arm, her small hand looking frail. "You always were my observant one, Patrick, and it's so sweet you're watching over your brothers."

Yeah, that was him. *Sweet*. His brothers might be heading toward the eye of the hurricane, all of them, but at least they were going forward. On the other hand, he was sitting alone in a bar booth near midnight having a nice chat with his mother and her sixty-year-old sister. "They'll be okay." He gave his mom the answer she needed.

"What about you?" she asked.

He sighed. "I'll be okay, too."

His mom cleared her throat. "Honey? Why are you here alone instead of out with Marisol tonight?" Aunt Alice turned to look down her nose at him and wait for an answer.

Because Marisol had to work and take care of her siblings, and she didn't want or need any help doing so. "She's busy."

"She needs you," Alice murmured.

"Marisol doesn't need anybody." And that was the rub. He was a guy who got things done, and he liked helping out. He liked figuring out problems, and he had a good head for it, which is why he'd become an EMT. Give him a crisis and he was the guy. "She definitely doesn't need me." They'd been friends forever, and he wanted more. A lot more.

His mom sighed. "Any woman would be lucky to have you, sweetheart. I think Marisol needs you, but she has so much going on, you know? It's hard to just stop and look around when you're in full motion. She quit college to take care of her siblings when their parents died." Her gaze moved to the pregnant Ginny Moreno, who was Marisol's younger sister. "She's such a saint."

She didn't kiss like a saint. Nope. Marisol Moreno kissed like a full-blooded woman who wanted to sin with the right guy—and damned if Patrick didn't want to be that man. Hell, his entire body tightened each time he thought about his lips over hers.

The door banged open, and Dakota Alvarez stormed into the bar. She wore a tight see-through shirt showing a bra that pushed up impressive looking breasts, a whole lot of makeup, and a skirt short enough Patrick could see a flash of red panties.

He watched as Joanne took in her daughter with wide eyes, and a scowl crossed Marcus's face when he saw his sister. Both of them pushed away from their seats.

"She is such trouble," his mom murmured quietly.

Yeah, but a whole world of hurt lived in her big, brown eyes. Patrick wondered why nobody else could see it. He made to move from the booth and intercede.

His mom stopped him with a hand on his arm. "I know you're the mediator around here, but I think you should let her family handle the situation."

It looked like the woman needed somebody in her corner, but his mom was right. It wasn't his place.

Dakota put both hands on her hips and surveyed the bar at large, her gaze stopping at Patrick, and then moving on. "Has anybody seen my dad?"

She looked tough and pissed, but her voice quavered. Every other night or so, she did the rounds of bars in the area looking for her dad, who was long gone by now. Hopefully.

Joanne reached her and grasped her arm, her eyes worried. "Dakota, he's gone. Let's go get coffee."

Dakota jerked free. "He left because of you."

Joanne paled, and Dillon crossed around the bar.

Marcus shook his head at Dillon and approached his sister. "This isn't the time or place. Let's go."

"You don't understand," Dakota all but yelled. "He left because of her. It's her fault."

Marcus spun her around toward the door. "You're done now."

She pulled free. "I'm an adult, Marcus. Fuck off."

"Then act like an adult and wear some clothes," Marcus threw back, his lips tight. "You look like a—"

"Marcus." His mom stopped his words cold.

"Like what?" Dakota turned around and advanced on her brother, fury bursting across her pretty face. "What?"

He glanced down at her short skirt. "Like a cheap whore."

Gasps echoed from down the bar.

"I wish you would've stayed in Montana," Dakota yelled, turning on a high red heel and stomping back outside.

Joanne went to follow her, and Marcus stopped her with a hand around her elbow. "Let her go. She's mad and needs to cool off."

"I want to go home," Joanne said, her lip trembling.

Marcus nodded and slipped an arm around her shoulder. "I'll take you home, Mom." Glancing to the side, he nodded at Brittany. "I'll be back in ten."

The sweet blonde nodded and stayed perched on her stool as Marcus helped his mom out the door.

Patrick kept his eye on Dillon, not liking the frustration etched across his face. Yep, there was definitely a storm coming.

But for now, he had to work early in the morning and needed to get home. Tipping back the rest of his beer, he scooted from the booth and placed his glass on the counter. His mom followed him, and after giving her a peck on the cheek and waving to his family, he loped out the door. Might as well get some sleep while he could.

He jumped into his Dodge pickup and swung out of the lot, heading down Cedar Street and out of town. The night was calm with a brilliant display of stars glimmering high above. He drove quietly, his mind turning over problems ranging from his brothers' love lives to his own. If he were in a different place with Marisol, he'd drop by her house for a tangle or at least a couple of kisses. Instead, he drove toward his home near the lake.

Something caught his eye, a glint of metal up ahead, and he slowed down.

An older Jeep Cherokee edged off the side of the road, its front in a series of bushes, its tail lights glowing a bright red. The driver's door was open, and the interior lights showed an empty seat. Crap. It was Luis Moreno's car.

Patrick pulled over and jumped from the truck. "Luis?"

The sound of retching echoed back from the other side of the vehicle.

His heartbeat kicking up, Patrick hustled around the rear of the Jeep to see Luis bent over, puking up his guts. The stench of vomit and alcohol slammed into him, and he coughed, partially turning away. "Luis?"

Luis finished throwing up and slowly straightened, wiping his mouth on the sleeve of a dark T-shirt. "I'm dying," he gasped, turning around, tears in his eyes.

Patrick bit back a laugh. "What did you drink?"

"White Lightning." Luis hiccupped.

Patrick sobered and moved toward the kid, lowering his head. "How much?" The stuff was 200 proof, and it could kill.

"Only a couple of drinks, but it was e-e-nough." Luis turned and vomited again.

Patrick swiped both hands down his face. "And you tried to drive?" Anger began to filter through his veins.

Luis nodded and turned back around. "Home isn't far."

"You dipshit." Patrick lost any sense of sympathy. "Your sister is dealing with Ginny being pregnant, with running the bakery, and with pretty much being perfect, and you go and try to get yourself killed?" His voice rose on the end.

Luis hung his head. "I wasn't thinking. Mallory hates me."

Patrick closed his eyes, trying for patience. Of course it was about a girl. Wasn't it always about a girl? He sighed and reopened his eyes. "Get in my truck. If you're gonna puke again, jump out."

Luis staggered and looked at his Jeep. "I can't leave—"

"Get in the truck or I'm calling my brother to come help. You know? My brother Dillon? The sheriff?"

Luis winced and turned to stumble toward the truck.

Shaking his head, Patrick strode around and jumped into the Jeep to turn it parallel to the road and lock it up. It'd be safe enough for the night.

He took the keys and hustled back to slide into his truck. Luis sat quietly, his head back, his eyes closed. Patrick slid down the windows to help with the stink. "Your sister is going to kill you." Yeah, he was feeling sympathy again.

"Don't tell her. Please don't tell her," Luis begged, not opening his eyes.

"Okay," Patrick said easily. "I won't say a word." He bit back a grin. Then he cleared his voice. "Want to tell me why you're ruining a perfectly good liver over a girl?" Not that he hadn't just been doing the same thing.

Luis shrugged. "I love Mallory Alvarez. Lacey Salt made a pass at me, tried to get naked, and I kissed her. But I *stopped*. I really stopped. But Mal found out, and now she just wants to be friends."

Ah, hell. Patrick didn't want to overstep any bounds with Marisol, but the kid sounded desperate. "Does Mallory believe you?"

"Yes," Luis sighed. "And she didn't like it tonight when Lacey started flirting with me."

"I'm the last guy you should probably take advice from, but it sounds like you just need to romance Mallory a little. Flowers and cupcakes." Patrick rubbed his chin. Ah, to be back in high school again. Then he'd know what to do.

Luis leaned forward, his hand on his gut. "You think?"

"Yeah."

"Thanks." He shivered. "You're totally into my sister, huh?"

Patrick blinked. "Yeah."

"That's cool."

Was it? Too bad Marisol didn't think so. Enough of the feeling sorry for himself crap. They entered the residential area, and he pulled into the driveway of a tiny but well maintained bungalow. A porch light was on, and the second gravel crunched under his tires, Marisol threw open the door.

Light framed her from behind. She wore yoga pants and a threadbare T-shirt decorated with a faded picture of the Cookie Monster eating several snickerdoodles.

As Patrick jumped from the truck, he had the oddest thought that the Monster only liked chocolate chip.

Luis dropped out of the passenger side and kept on going until he hit the gravel.

Marisol cried out and ran from the porch, her dark hair flying behind her.

Patrick reached him first and yanked him up. "He's fine."

Marisol skidded to a stop with a wince. "He is not fine. Luis?"

Luis tried to straighten up. "I'm, er, fine, sis." His voice slurred the entire sentence.

She reared back. "You're *drunk?*"

Nope. Patrick hadn't had to say a word, just like he'd promised.

Luis swayed. "No. I'm, ah…"

"Drunk," Marisol spat, her eyes wide. "Are you kidding me? Did you drive?"

Patrick winced. "Let's get him into bed before he passes out, shall we?" They'd have to keep an eye on the kid through the night, but it was unlikely he'd sipped enough to have alcohol poisoning.

Marisol nodded, her bare feet scrunching in the gravel.

Patrick bit back annoyance. "Get inside before you cut your feet, Marisol. I've got Luis."

She shook her head, reaching for her brother.

"Now." Patrick was done playing nice.

She jerked, and her mouth dropped open as she looked at him. Yeah. He'd never been anything but cajoling and gentle with her, and so far, that hadn't worked any. If the woman thought he was going to sit there and watch her cut her feet up for no reason, she didn't know him at all.

With a huff that was nothing short of adorable, she turned and jumped onto the grass before stomping for the porch.

"Yer in troooble, maaan," Luis slurred, leaning against Patrick.

"Look who's talking." Patrick slid a shoulder under Luis's arm and all but hefted him across the driveway. The kid had obviously been working out over the summer, and he weighed a ton. Finally, they stumbled into the house.

Older but well maintained furniture made up the living room, which was spotless and dotted with knickknacks from years ago. The walls needed to be painted, and Patrick would love to dig in, but Marisol would take his offer the wrong way.

"Please stay. I'll be out in a minute." Marisol took over then, ushering Luis across the comfortable living room to the back of the house, where her voice became a soothing hum.

Patrick shut the door and crossed inside to take a seat on the sofa, turning off the television and pushing a bright yellow crocheted blanket to the side. If he and Marisol were going to talk, he wanted her full attention.

She came out, her eyes dark, lines cutting into the side of her mouth. "Where did you find him?"

"On the road from the lake. He drank moonshine, but since he puked most of it out, he'll be all right. Just check on him throughout the night." Patrick tilted his head. "Come sit by me, Mari."

Her hands fluttered together, but she moved forward to sit next to him. "Thank you for picking him up. He was driving." She sighed and glanced down at her knees. "I taught him better."

The woman was always blaming herself and finding fault with her skills as a guardian. Patrick shook his head. "This isn't your fault. It's normal and unfortunate behavior for an idiot teenaged boy. Believe me, my mom has tons of stories."

Red tinged Marisol's cheeks. "If you say so." She glanced at the clock. "It's late, Patrick."

Yeah. It was definitely late. He'd wanted to have this talk with her over a nice dinner, but here they were, and he was tired of being in limbo. So he turned, grasped her arms, and settled her on his lap.

She teetered, both hands going to his chest. "What in the world are you doing?"

"This." Sliding his hand in her hair, he tilted her head and covered her mouth with his.

CHAPTER 3

Marisol's mouth opened in surprise, and Patrick took full advantage, sweeping his tongue inside. Warmth and sparks lit through her, and her mind spun. The grip on her neck was gentle and yet somehow firm, holding her in place.

The feeling of somebody else taking control, of having just a minute to feel and not think, swept through her along with need. Definite need that went way beyond want. Sitting on his lap felt right, and for the first time in so long, she felt protected.

He took her mouth, kissing her like he'd never stop. Her hands flattened against the strong muscles in his chest, while the firm thighs beneath her held her safe. There was so much hardness to his body that his gentleness seemed all the more impressive. Sexy and sure, he took the kiss deeper.

Her nipples peaked, and heat burned through her. She kissed him back, free for the tiniest of moments. All of a sudden, she wasn't an overworked businesswoman or a struggling older sister. She was all woman.

Patrick Murphy's woman.

A low groan came from the back bedroom, jerking her from the moment. She yanked her mouth free and listened, trying to hear above their ragged breathing. Nothing. Luis was all right.

She'd forgotten her intoxicated brother in the moment of passion. What had she been doing? Embarrassment straightened her spine one vertebra at a time. She drew away, and Patrick let her.

Lust glittered in his light blue eyes, and desire darkened his skin. A question, almost a demand, lived on his chiseled face.

If she said yes, they'd be in bed in a second. Naked and learning everything about each other.

God, her body wanted her to say yes. But she knew better. Her sister was pregnant, her brother was now drinking and driving, and she was responsible for them. For raising them. Frankly, she was doing a pretty shitty job.

She pushed against his chest. "I—I—can't."

He lifted an eyebrow. "It feels like you really can."

She snorted a laugh. How could he be funny when they were both in pain? Taking a shuddering breath, she pushed away to sit next to him. "Patrick, I can't start something romantic right now." It wasn't like he was asking for marriage, and she couldn't blame him, but she couldn't just start sleeping around. Not when she had her siblings to take care of. What kind of example would that be?

"You want me." No ego and only fact leveled his tone.

She nodded. Why lie? "I do, but I can't afford the complication right now. I mean, I don't know." Could she be any more wishy-washy?

He turned and lifted her chin.

Okay. She was liking this new take-charge attitude of his, and her girly parts needed to calm the hell down.

"Ah, Marisol. This feels so right, don't you think?" He ran a thumb over her bottom lip.

The words caught in her throat because nothing had ever felt better. The idea of what he could do with his entire body for a whole night sent a shudder through her. Would she be enough for him? It wasn't like she had tons of experience. A guy like Patrick had probably been with some pretty amazing women. "I need to take care of my brother tonight," she said, the words sounding beyond lame.

Patrick nodded, released her, and stood. "It has been a long night, and you have Luis to deal with in the morning. But pretty soon, you and I need to have a serious talk."

She stood, her knees shaky. Patrick was either all in or all out, and she knew it. He saw the world in clear lines, and whatever she told him, he'd take as the truth and go with it. "I know." Her heart actually hurt, but she needed time to figure out the right words. What should she do?

He stood so tall and sure—so strong. Dark hair, intelligent eyes, a definite hero in a modern world. His brothers had chosen law and the military, while he'd chosen to be an EMT right at home to help people. In a crisis, there was nobody better than Patrick Murphy. The previous month, one elderly woman in town waited to call an ambulance after fracturing her ankle until she knew Patrick was on duty. He was that good.

Why couldn't they just wait a few years for when Luis was in college, and she could really be free? But with Ginny and the new baby, would Marisol ever really be free? Ginny might be heading for a fall if Logan decided he wanted out, and what then? Marisol would have to once again pick up the pieces.

It wasn't fair to ask a guy like Patrick to wait. But could she take a chance with him now?

As she walked him to the door, her body felt heavy. What was she going to do?

He paused. "Keep an eye on Luis, and if you need me, call me. He should be fine." Without touching her again, Patrick strode for his truck, not turning around, and she had a sudden vision of her life if she let him go. Alone and lonely.

Sighing, she turned and locked the door, allowing the silence of the night to tick around her. What would it be like to live with a man? With Patrick? She'd been in her third year of college when her parents had died, so she'd quit to come home and raise her siblings.

She'd never lived with a man.

Sure, she'd had a couple of boyfriends before her parents had died, but nothing really serious. Could somebody forget how to have sex? The thought made her chuckle.

Sex with Patrick would be amazing—she just knew it. But being with him would mean more than multiple orgasms.

What would it be like to have somebody to talk to every day, to share problems with? Doubts crept in, like always. If she wasn't enough for her siblings, and based on how crappy they were doing, she sucked…how could she be enough for a man like Patrick?

She hustled in to check on her brother. He sprawled across the bed, snoring softly into his pillow, so big and strong all of a sudden. When had he grown so much? Soon he wouldn't need her at all—if he got his life back on track.

Drinking moonshine was one of the stupidest things he'd ever done. The fact that he'd then driven his truck afterward made her nauseated. What if he'd hit a tree? Or another car? What if it had been Dillon

Murphy, the sheriff, who'd found Luis? Her kid brother would be in jail right now facing a DUI charge.

Yet as he slept, she couldn't help but remember the sweet, curly-haired toddler who'd followed her around every day, happy to just be with her. What had happened to that little boy?

Closing the door, she went back to the couch and turned the TV on. Since she'd have to check on Luis every couple of hours, just to make sure, she might as well sleep there.

A vehicle in the driveway caught her attention, and she jumped up. Was Patrick back? Her heart ripped into action and butterflies winged through her abdomen. If he'd returned, would she say no again? Her body still hummed from his kiss. She'd never wanted anybody like she did him. Throwing open the door, she gaped as Ginny stepped out of Logan's truck and made her way to the door.

"Hi, sis," Ginny said, turning to wave at Logan.

Marisol blinked. "Ginny. What are you doing here?" She winced. "I didn't mean—"

Ginny turned and maneuvered by her and inside. "I know what you meant. I just wanted to see you."

Marisol's heart swelled. She swallowed and shut the door. "I'm so glad to see you, too, but it's after midnight. Shouldn't you be sleeping?"

"Probably, but sometimes I get tired of resting, you know?"

Marisol nodded. Hope tried to flare inside her. "Are you moving back home with us?"

"I don't think so." Ginny walked around to sit in an easy chair, rubbing her barely protruding belly. "I was out with Logan, and it's late, so I didn't want to wake the Salts. I told them I'd probably stay here tonight."

Expectant moms shouldn't be out so late, but Marisol wasn't going to lecture and risk Ginny storming off. For the first time in too long, all three of them were under the same roof, although Luis was pretty much passed out. Warmth infused Marisol, and she hustled around the couch to fetch the yellow blanket and fold it over Ginny's legs. "Can I get you anything to eat? Are you hungry?"

"No, thanks." Ginny kicked off her sandals and put her feet on the coffee table. "I just needed a break from the Salts and their hovering. I mean, I like having a family watch out for me and the baby, but sometimes it's too much."

Pain sliced into Marisol. "You have a family here."

Ginny blinked and softened her voice. "I know, but it's different there."

Of course it was. Celeste was a real mom and knew how to take care of people. So far, all Marisol was doing was screwing up life for her siblings. She'd had no clue how to raise them. She sat on the sofa and turned down the television show. "How are things with Logan?"

Ginny smiled and all of a sudden looked carefree. "They're good. Really good. In fact, his family reminds me of the Salts, you know? They're so supportive."

Unease ticked down Marisol's spine. "I'm sure they are. But Ginny, you can't just trade one family for another." Yet wasn't that what Ginny had already done once?

Ginny frowned. "I'm not. But I have a future to think about and need to do the right thing for this baby."

A future with Logan? Already? Sure, them dating was okay, but talking about forever so soon? Marisol smoothed her hands down her yoga pants. "Do you see Logan as your future?"

"Maybe." Ginny's face turned thoughtful. "I mean, we both feel lost a lot, but when we're together, we kind of find each other." She laughed, the sound a little strained. "It sounds weird, but it feels right."

There wasn't a way to argue about that. "Are the Salts okay with you already dating?"

"They say they are," Ginny said slowly, her gaze dropping to her slim feet. "But I don't know. They see Jacob in this baby, and they lost him, so they're holding on tight."

Marisol sat up, her instincts humming. "That's understandable. I mean, it's Jacob's baby, and now you're living with them. They have earned a place in the baby's life."

Ginny flushed. "I know, and they'll be great grandparents, I'm sure. I think Celeste is as maternal as Logan's mom," she added, referring to Sonya Murphy. "So if I need help, they're there."

"I'm there, too."

Ginny blinked. "Oh, I know. But you're not a mom, Marisol. You'll be a great aunt."

Ouch. Just how badly had she failed through the years? Ginny had always resented her acting like a mother instead of a sister, but even so, Marisol had tried. "So you're really doing all right?"

Ginny's chin firmed, and a strong light entered her brown eyes. "I am, and for the first time since the accident, I feel like I'm doing the right thing. That I'm on the right path."

Marisol frowned, the hair standing up on the back of her neck. Something wasn't right in the statement, but she couldn't track it down. "What aren't you telling me?"

Ginny's eyes opened wide. "Nothing. You know everything."

Marisol stared at her sister. More was going on with Ginny than she knew, and she just couldn't figure it out. She bit her lip. "How are you feeling about Jacob?" It had been a surprise to learn that Ginny and Jacob had been dating. Then having him die in the car accident had nearly destroyed Ginny. The poor girl had been driving.

"I miss him." Ginny picked at the blanket, her voice cracking. "It's not just losing Jacob, you know? I've lost a possible future—one I really wanted. What we could've had."

Tears pricked Marisol's eyes, and she reached out to rub her sister's shoulder. "I get that. What about the nightmares? They still terrible?"

Ginny sighed. "I still have them, but they're not as bad since I started talking to Logan about them. He has nightmares about Afghanistan, and he shares those, so it's like we're helping each other to heal." She leaned forward. "He's so strong, and he makes me feel safe. It's nice to feel…"

"Protected?" Marisol murmured, flashing back to the moment on the sofa where Patrick had held her close and made her wish for so much more.

"Yeah." Ginny's lip curved. "Logan will stand between me and any danger, even town gossips, and I like that. Whether or not I should, I don't know."

"You should." Marisol smiled. "He's a good man."

"Yeah. He is." Ginny's smile slid away. "I don't deserve him." Something buzzed in her pocket, and she drew out a new smart phone to answer. "Hi, Celeste. Yes, I'm fine. Yes, I'm with Marisol, and we're just catching up. Please stop worrying." She paused and shook her head at Marisol. "Okay. Goodnight." She clicked off and shoved the phone in her pocket. "I hate worrying her, but I just wanted to come home."

Marisol stood, concern filtering through her. While she liked this new independence of Ginny's, it might just be a *dependence* on Logan, and what if something went wrong between them? "Is Celeste all right?"

"Yes." Ginny groaned and pushed to her feet. "She's just concerned, but I'm okay. Or I will be."

Marisol glanced down. "That's a nice new phone." A very expensive phone.

"Celeste bought it for me so she could get ahold of me whenever." Ginny blanched. "I shouldn't have taken it, I know. In fact, I told her that I couldn't accept the phone, but she got so upset—"

"Oh, Ginny." Marisol studied her sister. "It's okay, you know? You don't have to worry so much about everyone else."

Ginny threw up her arms. "I know, but I feel like…" She blushed and then covered her face before taking several deep breaths. Finally, her hands dropped. Her lips trembled, but she smiled. "It's just hormones. I'll be okay, I promise. Sleep will help." She leaned over and placed a soft kiss on Marisol's cheek before turning for the back bedrooms. "I'll talk to you tomorrow. Night."

Marisol watched her disappear around the corner, her temples pounding. Her family was out of control, and she had absolutely no idea how to fix things. Outside, thunder began to roll across the sky, and soon rain bombarded the earth. It was a minor storm, nothing big.

She knew, somehow deep in her gut, that a much bigger storm was on the way. God help them all.

CHAPTER 4

Her family was a bunch of asshats. Dakota Alvarez drove recklessly out of town, pissed beyond belief after leaving Murphy's Pub. Just who did Marcus think he was? The bastard had done nothing but desert them the first chance he got, and now he came home and sided with their pathetic mother?

Somehow that woman had made their father leave. Dakota just knew it.

She tried to tug down the too-short skirt on the leather seat and then just gave up. A whore, huh? Forget Marcus. Someday she was going to be a senator's wife, and then everybody could just kiss her ass. They had no clue who she could be.

She pulled over and dialed the senator's phone.

No answer.

Fury roared through her. Of course, he was busy, but lately…she'd felt him moving away. His concentration seemed to be somewhere else.

He was running for reelection, so maybe he was worried about it. The man was smart and powerful, so she didn't see why he'd be concerned.

But a niggling doubt wouldn't leave her stomach. Marcus had deserted the family the second he could get out of town. Her father had left, for whatever reason, and she was all alone. After everything she'd shared with the senator, he couldn't abandon her, too. She wouldn't let him. So she turned the phone around and sent him a quick text message, saying that if he didn't answer her, she was going by his house.

Just how would his perfect, boring, old wife feel about that?

He answered immediately, and triumph roared right through her until she read the text. Oops.

I'M NOT A MAN YOU THREATEN.

She winced and quickly began to type. I KNOW, AND I'M SORRY. IT'S BEEN A CRAPPY NIGHT, AND I NEED YOU.

Several seconds ticked by. Finally, a text came in.

I'M VERY BUSY.

Hell, it was after midnight. How busy could he be? Her hands grew sweaty and she wiped them on the cheap skirt before starting to type. IF YOU CARE AT ALL, YOU'LL MEET ME TONIGHT. I'LL MAKE IT WORTH YOUR WHILE.

Silence. More silence. Thunder clapped above the car, and she jumped. Finally, her phone lit up.

IT BETTER BE GOOD. MEET ME AT THE CABIN.

Her chest relaxed. Oh, he was still hers, and she needed to remind him how good they were together. All of his distance lately was just from business and from being married to the wrong woman. That boring twit didn't understand him and thus couldn't help ease his stress.

Dakota knew all about easing his stress because he'd taught her. She'd learned so much from him, and she knew she could give it all back. She could take care of him, could become his everything and still get the life she deserved. Balls, political fundraisers, and big houses with servants. It was exactly what her father would want for her.

Humming softly, she pulled back onto the road and drove around the lake, taking note of a large bonfire still crackling on the far shore. Must be the high school kids having a party. High school was only a couple of years behind her, but it felt like a lifetime ago. She was in an affair with a powerful man, and her future lay bright in front of her.

Finally.

She reached the cabin and drove around back to hide her car beneath a series of pine trees, just as he'd taught her. Being in the shadows was temporary for her, and soon she'd be in the limelight. She could make Sebastian so proud of her, and once she was living in mansions, she'd let her dad come and stay with them. He'd worked so hard his entire life, and it'd be nice for him to take a break and relax.

She and the senator could do that for her dad.

Singing softly, she stepped onto the mud and then swore as her high heel dug in. Gripping the door handle, she yanked free and tried to tiptoe around the structure to the wide wooden porch fronting the lake. The interior was dark, so she was alone.

She took time to scrape off her heel and then sat on the rolling porch swing, her gaze across the lake at the bright fire. Several shapes danced around, but it was too far away for her to be able to identify anybody. Was her perfect sister, Mallory, there?

Dakota sniffed. Probably not. Mal was most likely at home studying algebra or something equally boring. Dork. Although, when Dakota became the senator's wife, she'd be nice to her sister and invite her to visit their mansion. If Mal stopped being such a judgmental wench, of course.

Not their mother. That witch could shrivel and die. The clumsy oaf had somehow convinced half the town that Hector Alvarez was a wife-beater, and that couldn't be further from the truth. Now that he was gone, Joanne actually seemed happy and was even wearing makeup. She hadn't tripped or fallen once. Those injuries had probably been self-created just so Joanne could blame Hector and make the townspeople hate him.

Dakota would make such a better wife than Joanne ever had.

Rain began to patter down around her, and she hugged herself, dry under the porch roof. Finally, a car purred down the lane, its lights off.

Her breath sped up.

Sebastian's BMW crawled by the cabin and parked in the back. Seconds later, he strode through the rain, so tall and powerful her heart just stopped. "Get inside," he said, moving past her and pushing open the door.

She faltered. Her throat clogged, and she followed him inside, waiting until he'd drawn all the drapes and turned on the kitchen light. "I'm sorry—"

He turned around suddenly, anger in his brown eyes. "You threatened me."

She wrinkled her nose. "I didn't mean it."

He didn't speak and just studied her with no expression on his face.

The rain increased in strength, and she tried to hold his gaze, but she gave up and looked around. God, she loved the cabin. The main room held a heavy maple table that could fit about sixteen people, a fancy kitchen with stainless steel appliances, and a gathering room with plush chairs and the biggest stone fireplace she'd ever seen. Finally, when the silence was louder than the storm, she turned back to him. "I'm sorry. If you let me, I can make it up to you." Her voice turned flirty at the end.

His face softened, and a new tension filtered through the room.

"What in the world are you wearing?" His gaze raked her.

Heat filled her face, and she tried to tug down the skirt. "Um, I thought you'd like it." Maybe Marcus had been right. "Do I look, I mean, like a whore?" Fear quaked down her skin on the heels of vulnerability. She shuffled her feet. One of her heels was still dirty.

He slowly smiled.

Her heart turned over.

"No, you look incredibly sexy." His voice lowered to a guttural tone.

She grinned, the entire world brightening. Yeah. She was sexy, and everything was going to be all right. "Thank you." She took him in. Pressed black slacks, blue golf shirt, also pressed, and impressive muscles shifting beneath both. He worked out regularly, and his body was nicely cut. His salt and pepper hair made him look intelligent and rich. "You're the sexy one here."

He lifted an eyebrow. "Don't ever threaten me again."

She nodded, pushing out her breasts. "I won't." Fluttering her eyelashes, she pretended to glance at his pockets. "No present for me tonight?"

He slowly shook his head. "Bad girls who threaten me do not get a present."

She stuck out her lower lip. "It feels like you're not interested in me anymore, Sebastian." Her eyes widened, and she stiffened. Why had she said that? She needed to be smooth and not needy. A man like him would be turned off by neediness.

He crossed his arms. "You're a grown-up, and you need to act like it. My job is demanding, and you know it." Disappointment turned down his lips. "Or maybe you can't handle a real man and should go back to boys."

Hurt pierced through her more at the disappointment than the harsh words. She slowly began to unbutton her tight shirt, gratified when his eyes flared. Oh, he'd taught her well how to interest and then please him. She was back in control. "I can handle you."

"Prove it," he said.

* * * *

Sebastian watched her fingers tremble as she unbuttoned the white shirt to fully show the red bra that had already been on display. He'd lied, of course. She definitely looked like a whore. Not like the new intern his mother had just hired for the campaign staff.

That girl was barely eighteen with soft eyes and even softer skin. When he'd shaken her hand earlier, he'd almost come in his pants. Her blush had been so pretty and innocent, he hadn't been able to get her out of his mind. When he had her, and he surely would, he might even be her first.

For now, the girl shrugging her shirt to the floor caught his attention again. Dakota was stunning, and oh, so willing. A pretty blonde with serious daddy issues Sebastian had taken full advantage of. But he'd about used her up, and his attention would soon wander.

Not tonight, though.

Tonight he'd finish what they'd started and get everything he wanted.

She reached for the front clasp of her bra, and he held out a hand. "Wait."

Warmth and power rushed through him at how quickly she stilled. To think that this silly piece of ass had once rejected him with a laugh and a snarl.

Now he fucking owned her.

She watched him with wide eyes, desire and a desperate need darkening them to almost black.

"Turn around, slowly. Let me see every beautiful inch of you," he ordered.

Pleasure curved her lips, and she turned, arms at her sides. A flash of red from beneath her skirt caught his attention. "Take off your skirt."

She obeyed without question, dropping the flimsy material to the floor.

He breathed in, letting desire flow through him. She was truly beautiful in a trailer trash way, which is exactly how he wanted her to be. All of that lush, firm flesh only held briefly by the young. Plus, she was amazingly flexible. He'd thought Ginny Moreno had been flexible when he'd had her feet behind her ears, fucking her hard, but Dakota beat her hands down.

At the thought of Ginny and the bastard she carried, the kid that just *couldn't* be his, he frowned.

Dakota faltered. "Sebastian?"

He threw thoughts of Ginny and her baby into the abyss, where they both belonged, and concentrated on the desperate treat in front of him. "Don't stop," he said.

Dakota took a step away from the table, and he shook his head.

"The bedroom?" she asked, standing in all red. Red shoes, red panties, red bra. The color of sin.

"No. The table," he said, reaching for his shirt and drawing it over his head. Since it was merely a golf shirt and not one of his dress shirts, he tossed the material on the floor.

She swallowed and glanced back at the table. "I'm betting you never do your wife on a table."

He snorted. His wife was a stunning, older blonde he didn't *do* anywhere or any time. Except for the couple of times they'd had to screw to get kids, the woman didn't want anything sexual to do with him. "You're not my wife," he retorted.

Hurt filled her eyes, and she quickly blinked it away. "I mean more to you than she does."

He paused. Unease filtered through his lust. "My wife is the perfect politician's wife. I'm not leaving her. Ever." God, the girl had to get that, right?

Dakota's chin lifted. "If she was so perfect, you wouldn't need me so much. You'd be home with her, happy like you are with me."

Damn, the girl was stupid. The demand in her tone meant they had to end things soon. But there was still tonight, and he intended to make the drive out to the cabin worth his time. "You do make me happy, Dakota. Usually."

Her head jerked. "Usually?"

It was almost too easy. The time for seducing and building her up was over. She'd given him almost everything. Yet almost wasn't good enough for Sebastian Rush, even though he was already getting bored. "Yes. Usually. You're a sweet girl, but I'm a man who needs a woman. You have to know that."

Fire flashed in her big lonely eyes, and she ran her hands over her bra. "I am a woman."

His groin tightened. "Think so?" he murmured.

"Yes."

He released his belt and slowly drew it through the loops to drop onto the floor. "Think you can keep me?"

"I know I can." Confidence filtered through Dakota's voice in direct contrast to the wariness now in her posture. She clasped her hands together.

"All right. Turn around and bend over the table." He smiled, his lids half lowering.

She hesitated.

"Or go home," he finished.

Her mouth dropped open, she glanced at the door, and then her shoulders went down. She swallowed and turned to walk on the ridiculous heels to bend over, her cheek on the table, her face turned toward him. Her uncertainty did nothing but increase his desire.

"You want to be mine, Dakota?" he asked quietly.

"Yes." Her voice trembled.

"Good," he responded, unzipping his pants and crossing the distance between them.

CHAPTER 5

Marisol Moreno stepped out from under the shade of the giant oak tree in the center of town, shielded her eyes with her hand, and surveyed the group repairing every board in the gazebo in preparation of Founders' Day. The storm of the night before had passed over, leaving the air crisp and the ground damp. Even in the warming Texas sun, she shivered. "We need the ground to dry in time."

Her best friend, Tara Douglas, flipped open a page on her clipboard and made a huge checkmark. "Dry grass. Got it."

Amusement flittered through Marisol, and she grinned. "Smart aleck."

Tara chuckled and tossed curly brown hair over her shoulder. "Stop worrying. The day of the festival will be perfect. We have tons of folks volunteering to help get ready, and the weatherman assures me we'll have fine Texas weather for the next few weeks, with maybe just a couple of storms. So let's just relax a little."

A group of lawyers jogged down the courthouse steps over to the north and then turned to head toward the Cuppa Joe Bakery. It was a good thing that Lacey was at work today and ready to sell some muffins. Sales were a bit down, and Marisol had a mortgage to pay. But she'd promised to help with the Founders' Day preparations, so she'd had to leave work for a while.

The breeze picked up, and Tara shut her clipboard. "Let's go grab lunch at Bluebonnet."

Marisol glanced toward the gazebo and caught sighed of a dark head bent over, concentrating on hammering nails. Her heart began to pound faster. "Um, okay."

Tara followed her gaze. "Hmmm. Cute, right? My cousin gets tougher looking every time I see him. Has Patrick been working out?"

Heat slithered into Marisol's face. "How should I know?"

"Right." Tara turned and rolled her eyes. "You're the color of Hedda Garten's sofa with the crazy damask pillows. Are you two finally, you know?"

"No. We are not finally *you knowing*." Although last night, she'd really wanted to. Marisol began to turn just as Patrick stood up, his gaze slamming into hers. She took an involuntary step back.

"Wow," Tara whispered.

Wow, indeed. Marisol wanted to run, but her sensible tennis shoes remained glued to the spot. Patrick wore faded jeans across powerful legs and a blue T-shirt that brought out the stunning color of his eyes, even at that distance. His shoulders were wide, his chest broad, and just looking at him made her salivate. "He's not mine," she murmured.

"He could be," Tara countered, slipping an arm through Marisol's. "Either go over there and plant one on him, or let's go to lunch and talk about this issue of yours."

Marisol swallowed. "Lunch. Yeah. Let's do that." Yet even as she began to turn, she could feel his gaze remaining on her. So she lifted her head and allowed her friend to lead her out of the park and down the street to the cafe. Finally, when they were out of sight, she released the breath she hadn't realized she'd been holding.

"Man, you have it bad," Tara muttered as she pulled open the door to the cafe and ushered them both inside.

The smell of bacon and hamburgers filtered around, and Marisol led the way to a booth in the back. They both ordered their favorites from a teenager with purple streaks in her hair, and then Marisol took a deep drink from her sweating water glass.

"Talk," Tara said, her gray eyes serious in her strong, intelligent face.

Marisol shuddered. "Patrick wants more."

"No kidding. Geez."

Funny. "How can I give him more?" Marisol shook her head, tears pricking the back of her eyes. "I really care for him, I do. But right now, Ginny is pregnant, living with the Salts, and falling in love with Logan Murphy. And I swear, there's something going on with her I can't figure out. Something's wrong."

Tara lifted an eyebrow. "Something more than everything you just said?"

Heat rushed down Marisol's torso. Her ears burned. "Yeah. Maybe. I don't know. But I do know that I'm totally failing her, and my parents would be so disappointed."

Tara reached over the table and grabbed her hand. "That couldn't be further from the truth. Come on, Marisol. You gave up your entire life to raise those kids, and you're doing the best anybody could do. Give yourself a break."

"I can't," Marisol whispered, her stomach aching. She should have ordered something bland instead of the spicy chicken salad. "And Luis? For goodness sakes. He came home last night drunker than a wino on a binge, and it was from sucking down White Lightning."

Tara gasped and sat back. "Where in the heck did he get ahold of moonshine?"

"I don't know," Marisol admitted, failure all but eating her whole. "He was still snoring away this morning, and I let him sleep. Poor guy nearly puked up his liver last night."

Tara grimaced. "I bet he won't drink again."

Probably not. Marisol brightened a little. "Good point." She bit her lip. "I found condoms in his room, and he said they were just in case, but what do I know? He's a teenaged boy. I hope if he's having sex, he's using condoms, but considering he's also drinking moonshine these days, he might be having sex and *not* using them." She shuddered.

"Sounds like a normal teenaged boy and parent issue," Tara said softly.

Marisol took another drink of water, her throat dry. "I guess. But how can I handle them, keep the business going, and give Patrick any attention at all? I mean, I'm just not up to it."

Tara frowned. "Is that it, or are you afraid to take a chance?"

"What do you mean?"

"Well, you lost your parents young, and then you had tons of responsibility drop onto your shoulders. I mean, I can't blame you if you're afraid to get close to anybody again."

Marisol coughed. "That's not it." She couldn't meet Tara's eyes.

"Isn't it? What if you got together with Patrick, had a couple of adorable little blue-eyed babies that spoke Gaelic, and then he got hit by a bus? I mean, isn't that your biggest fear?" Tara unfolded her paper napkin and dropped the utensils on the table, her voice gentle and tentative. "It would be my fear if I were you."

Was that it? Was she just a big old wimp? "I don't know, Tara." Marisol scrubbed both hands down her face.

"Listen, I get it. Your self-esteem isn't that great right now, and part of that is Ginny's attitude toward you, which you can't help. Someday she'll understand how hard you've worked, but not now. Not yet." Tara sat back as the waitress deposited their salads.

Marisol reached for her fork. "I don't know what I'm going to do about Patrick, but I do know I'm tired of talking about it. How are you and Bryce doing?"

Tara took a deep breath. "Just fine. We're great."

Humor bubbled up through Marisol, and she let out a short chuckle. "Ah. *Fine*."

Tara rolled her eyes. "I know. Lame. I wish I could tell you how Bryce and I are doing, but I'm just not sure enough to even reach a conclusion there. Sometimes it's so hard."

Marisol nodded, guilt sweeping her again. Here she was going on and on about the hot Irish guy who wanted her in bed, and Tara was dealing with a struggling husband, an autistic son, and a daughter who was acting out for more attention. "Is Bryce dealing with everything better?"

Tara put down her fork. "I can't tell. I mean, on the surface, he's all smiles and assurances. Like he is in church with the congregation."

It seemed a minister like Bryce would be more honest with his wife, but Marisol didn't say that. "But underneath the smiles?" She could understand hidden layers since she had so many.

Tara drew in air through her nose. "I think he's hurting. I mean, he had this perfect idea of a family, and he can't relate to Danny. The autism has really thrown Bryce for a loop, and I can't help but wonder if he's mad at God. I mean, Bryce dedicated his life to God, and then this happens, and it's like he's feeling betrayed."

Marisol leaned back. "That sounds confusing on so many levels."

"I know," Tara whispered. "And I'm just guessing because he won't talk to me about it. Not any of it." Her voice shook, so she took a drink of water. "Or maybe I'm wrong and he's in love with leprechauns or obsessing about collecting garden flamingos." Her smile looked forced. "Who knows?"

"At least you have a huge extended family to lean on," Marisol offered, trying to find something positive.

"Yeah, but that seems to depress Bryce even more." Tara shook her head. "He only has his sister, and I have two protective brothers and devoted parents. My big family seems to remind him that he doesn't have much. Although he could have all of them if he just realized it."

"What about his family? I mean, what's the deal there?"

Tara shook her head. "He won't talk about it, although I know it was bad. Neither he nor Kristin will talk about their childhood or parents, and I've never pushed because I figured it was in the past."

Weird. Marisol smiled softly. "Our childhood was pretty great." She and Tara had become friends in the first grade, bonding over love of purple glitter. They'd remained friends, and when Marisol's parents had died, Tara had been right there to help. If only Bryce would turn around and see the strength in his wife, everything would work out. "You're a great mom, Tara." Those kids were so lucky to have her.

Tara smiled. "Right back at ya. Ginny and Luis are fortunate to have you as their older sister, and one day when they're all grown up, they'll understand that as much as I do."

A shadow fell across the table, and Celeste Salt hovered nearby wearing a pretty floral dress, wringing her hands. The soon-to-be grandmother appeared worried and like she'd had more than one sleepless night lately. "I'm so sorry to interrupt."

Marisol's stomach dropped, but she forced a smile and scooted over in the booth. "You could never interrupt, Celeste. Please sit down."

Celeste swallowed and gracefully took a seat. "I hate to bother you, but I'm quite worried about Ginny."

Marisol straightened. "Is she okay? I thought she went back to your house this morning."

Celeste nodded and patted Marisol's hand. "Yes, she did, and right now she's resting. But I'm concerned about her hanging out with Logan at Murphy's bar so late. Drunk men, cigarette smoke, and such can't be good for the baby. Or for Ginny."

Marisol's head began to ache. Celeste had recently lost her son, Jacob, and his only offspring was currently gestating inside Ginny. While she had the same misgivings, the need to defend her sister rose hard and fast within her. "I understand your concern, but Ginny is a young adult with a mind of her own."

"But she's not being safe," Celeste snapped. She jerked back, her eyes widening. "Oh my. I'm so very sorry for my curtness."

Marisol grasped her hand, her temples pounding. "I know, Celeste. I really do. Jacob is gone, and the baby is coming, and I know how much you already love your grandchild. But Ginny is the baby's mother, and while she appreciates your love and security, you have to let her live her life."

Celeste nodded. "I know, but it's just such a miracle. A real miracle."

Marisol smiled and squeezed. "A baby is always a miracle, and I'm so happy that something of Jacob will live on. Let's just relax and let Ginny find her way. She's the only one who can." If nothing else, Marisol could ease the way between Celeste and Ginny, even if Ginny would never fully trust Marisol.

Celeste's chin firmed, and her shoulders went back. She studied both women. Finally, she pushed from the booth. "You're so very right. Thank you. Bye, Tara." She turned and walked toward the door.

"Whew," Tara whispered. "You handled that perfectly."

Man, she hoped so. "Remember when our biggest problem was what shoes to wear to school?" Marisol asked.

"Or what notebook to buy for which class?" Tara returned, her eyes sparkling. "Yeah. I totally remember."

"Me too," Marisol said slowly, glancing out the window just as Patrick and his older brother strode by, talking and walking with ease. Her heart hurt, and her stomach clenched. "I miss the good old days."

CHAPTER 6

Tara Douglas left the unsettling lunch with her best friend and wandered down Third Street toward the Lutheran church, smiling and nodding at people she passed. Her family had been ranching on land near Storm for almost two centuries, and she knew almost everybody. These were her people and her home, and she couldn't imagine living anywhere else.

Her mind wandered as she relaxed, and she naturally turned left to walk a couple of blocks to the cemetery. The sun shone down, glimmering off headstones and giving a sense of tranquility to the sprawling area.

She'd never been afraid of the graveyard. For some reason, she'd always found comfort among the dead resting peacefully.

It was the living who weren't at rest.

A shadow, cast long by the Texas sun, caught her eye.

Bryce.

He stood, hands in pockets, staring down at a fresh grave. Dark jeans covered his legs down to boots, and an older golf shirt showed he'd been working at the gazebo earlier to help in preparations. He was usually in slacks and a button-down shirt, and she liked seeing him in casual wear.

He hadn't been casual in way too long.

The sun glinted off his reddish hair, giving him the look of a wayward Highlander. Her own true romance hero…sans the kilt. A frown drew his eyebrows together, yet other than the facial movement, he didn't seem to breathe, so intense was he staring at the grave marker.

Not for a second had she thought to find him there, but maybe she was meant to. Alone among the dead, maybe they could finally talk about the living. About their marriage. But she was smart, she understood people, and she knew that pushing was a bad idea. So she wouldn't push. She took a deep breath and walked onto the grass and between headstones until reaching his side. When had she started steeling herself to talk to her own husband and the father of her two children?

Her lip started to sting from her biting it, so she stopped. "Bryce?"

He jerked and then glanced her way. "Tara." He looked around and then back at her. At one time, he would've reached to tug her into his side. Today he left his hands in his pockets, seeming so much farther than a few feet away. "What are you doing here?"

She looked toward Jacob Salt's gravestone. "I had lunch with Marisol and then went for a walk." Jacob had been young and had died so tragically in a car accident with Ginny Moreno. "What are you doing here?"

Bryce shrugged. "I'm not sure. We finished pounding nails into the gazebo, and I figured I'd head over and check on Jacob. The kid had his entire life ahead of him." Pain and bewilderment echoed in his tone.

"I know." Tara hesitated in reaching out to her husband. An invisible wall, one that shimmered with an ache she could actually feel, stood between them.

He blinked. "Where are the kids?"

She cleared her throat. "My mom is watching them." She loved her kids, but it was nice to get out on her own once in a while. Having grown-up time with Marisol had been as much for her benefit as for her friend's. They were both struggling, and they needed each other.

Bryce lowered his chin. "That's a lot for Alice to handle. Danny was out of control more than usual this morning."

Actually, it was their four-year-old, Carol, who seemed out of control. Danny was autistic, and Carol seemed to be acting out because her brother was getting more attention. "My mom can handle the kids, Bryce. She's the elementary school principal and has seen it all."

He shook his head. "We have our own family."

Yeah, but it wasn't like he was home right now with the kids, was he? Tara dug deep for patience. "They're family, too, and they're your family now, if you'd just let them in."

He shrugged his shoulders forward.

Enough of that. Tara patted his arm. "Bryce? At some point, you're going to have to talk to me, you know."

He turned, his blue eyes focusing on her. Really focusing on her for the first time in so long. "I, ah. I know."

She smiled, the tension leaving her body. He was finally seeing her. Hope unfurled in her abdomen, and she tugged his arm until his hand freed. "Good." Taking his hand, she settled into his side and let him retreat for now. "What's on your agenda today, Pastor Douglas?"

He gave a half-smile. "We're supposed to start planning out the booths for the festival. Do you have time to design a corner or two?"

She nodded and followed him between the graves and onto the sidewalk. "I have a little time." For the moment, as they walked back to the park, she could almost believe everything was going to be all right. Glancing up at the blue sky and then toward the lake, she pushed down a frown.

Gray clouds, the dark and rolling kind, were heading their way.

* * * *

Patrick Murphy strode alongside his older brother after having grabbed a pizza for lunch. They'd talked about the bar, their parents, and the Founders' Day events. Dillon was on duty, but not much was going on in the town, so he'd been able to stay through a dessert of cinnamon sticks. As was typical, they'd fought over the last one. Patrick thought that one had tasted the best of them all—or maybe it was just the thrill of a victory.

Now they headed down Second Street toward Storm Oak and the gazebo to see how the various repairs and cleanup in preparation for the upcoming celebration were going, their strides about even since they'd reached the same six-foot plus height in high school.

"Mom wants me to talk to you about Marisol," Dillon said, his lips turning in a grimace, his boots clomping on the concrete.

Patrick tripped and then caught himself. "You're kidding."

"Nope." Dillon's long stride didn't slow. Today he wore faded jeans, a black button-down shirt, and a badge and gun at his hip. Even the black cowboy hat on his head made him look like a Texas lawman from years ago. "So I'm talking."

Patrick snorted and shoved up the sleeves of his T-shirt. "You are such a dork."

"You're the dork," Dillon returned without heat as he waved to a couple of football players on the opposite sidewalk. "Seriously, what's going on?"

"I don't know. I like her, she likes me, but she won't take a chance." Patrick shoved his hands in his pockets. He wanted to be frustrated, but he could always see both sides of any issue, and he understood her position and need to protect herself.

Dillon cleared his throat. "Mom was, ah, worried about the way you looked at Dakota Alvarez last night."

Patrick jerked his head. "What? That's crazy."

"Is it?" Dillon murmured. "I mean, that's a girl who needs saving. Marisol works herself to death and needs saving. You, my brother, are a guy who tries to save everybody."

Heat burned to the tips of Patrick's ears. "That's the dumbest thing I've ever heard."

"Really? Come on, Patrick. I grew up with you and every dog, chicken, bird, and injured cat you brought home. And kids. Kids who needed food or just warmth."

Well, crap. He wasn't some do-gooder trying to save the world. It's just if a bird had a broken wing, he'd taken it home to heal. "I have no interest in Dakota and just felt sorry for her. The only person who can save her is, well, her." He shook his head and knew he shouldn't mention that it was Dillon's fault Dakota was so upset about her father deserting her. "Marisol is different. I have feelings for her, and I want to be with her. Not save her." Of course, if he was with her, he could certainly lighten her burden.

"Uh huh," Dillon said as they crossed by the savings and loan. "If you say so."

Temper, rare and unexpected, roared through Patrick. "Look who's talking," he muttered.

"Huh?"

"Joanne Alvarez? You know, the woman whose husband you ran out of town. Who's really trying to be a savior here?" Patrick asked.

Dillon winced. "Shut up."

"You shut up," Patrick returned in true brotherly style.

Dillon sighed. "Listen. I know I'm the last guy in the world who should give dating advice, but at some point, you have to shit or get off the pot."

Patrick shook his head. "Am I having bowel problems in this

scenario?"

"God." Dillon took off his hat and hit his leg with it. "You are so dense. What I mean is that you and Marisol either have to make a go of it or you need to move on. Find somebody to get serious with and give Mom some damn grandkids. She's done waiting."

"You give her grandkids," Patrick hissed, forcing a smile for Celeste Salt as she walked by wearing a dress with a bunch of flowers on it and looking like she was heading to church a couple of days early. "Wait a sec. If Ginny and Logan work out, she's having a kid. Mom will be a grandma. Problem solved."

Dillon glanced over his shoulder until Celeste was out of earshot. "You really think those two are going to work out? Ginny and Logan?"

"Sure. Why not?" Patrick hunched his shoulders. There were so many reasons why not, he felt like an idiot even asking the question. But he had his younger brother's back, and if Logan wanted Ginny, Patrick hoped to hell they got a happy ending.

"There are secrets and tragedies in that girl's eyes," Dillon said slowly. "She's not my business, but our brother is, and he has enough problems." Logan had recently returned from Afghanistan, and he definitely wasn't the same carefree guy who'd left town a few years ago. "I know sometimes he goes for a run in the middle of the night just to avoid sleeping."

Yeah, after midnight on a day last week, Patrick had been on a call to a small house fire, and he'd seen Logan in jogging clothes, watching the happenings. "Maybe he needs to run for a while."

"Maybe. But he's trying to save that girl when he should be saving himself."

Patrick stepped over a puddle. "Perhaps they can save each other."

"I hope so."

Patrick nodded as the reality of their lives smacked him between the eyes. "You know, it's a wonder Mom and Pops don't drink. A lot."

Dillon scoffed. "They own a pub. Of course they drink a lot. Can you blame them?"

Patrick grinned. "Pops drinks. Mom meddles."

"Both vices," Dillon said, digging an elbow into his ribs. "What am I supposed to report back to Mom about you?"

That was a fair question and one he'd been asking himself a lot lately. He'd wanted to give Marisol time to trust him and see that they would work out, but after he'd kissed her now a couple of times, it was becoming agony to be around her. "Do you have to report back?"

"Of course. You know Mom. What should I tell her?"

"That I'm going to either fish or cut bait," Patrick returned, using a much nicer metaphor than his brother had. It was time to force Marisol to make a decision, and he'd live with whatever decision she made. But he hoped, against all logic, that she'd choose to jump into the fire with him. Because she was a sweet woman who could use a little saving, and he was just the guy for the job.

They reached the gazebo, and he stopped short at seeing the woman of the conversation just arriving by the gazebo, immediately giving directions to a group of high schoolers. She wore cute Capris and a shimmery blouse, looking fresh and lovely.

She was so pretty with her black hair and even darker eyes. Every time he saw her, he took a sucker punch to the gut.

Dillon stopped next to him. "Man, you have droopy love eyes."

"Yeah," he agreed. He'd never lied to his brother and saw no reason to start now.

She pointed to something on top of the gazebo, and several of the kids nodded, keeping their gaze on her. Even the goofy high school boys paid attention to her, seeing something special.

Patrick's shoulders went back. His brother was right.

It was time to start a future…or get his heart broken. Either way, he was done waiting.

CHAPTER 7

After a long day of preparing for the festival and then working her bakery, Marisol handed over the box of cupcakes to Celeste, careful not to smudge the glass countertop. The room was empty save for the two of them, and darkness was beginning to fall outside. "These are Ginny's favorite."

Celeste smiled and gingerly reached for the box. "Thanks so much. I'm hoping she spends some time at home tonight." A flush worked its way up Celeste's fine cheekbones. "I mean, at our house. Your house is still her home. I mean—"

"It's okay," Marisol said quietly, wiping her hands on her apron. "I know what you mean." And Celeste was home all day, so she could take better care of Ginny during the pregnancy. Of course, Ginny was off with Logan more often than not now. "How are you and Travis doing?"

Celeste's eyes darkened. "We're hanging in there. Having the baby and Ginny to focus on really helps, but sometimes I pick up the phone to call our son, and then I remember he's gone."

Marisol's heart ached. She couldn't even imagine losing a child. "I'm so sorry."

Celeste's lips trembled, but she smiled. "Thank you. Travis is doing the best he can, but he's pretty much thrown himself into work again, and I can't blame him. It helps to be able to concentrate on anything else but Jacob, you know?"

Marisol nodded. She'd done the same thing when her parents had died and had focused solely on her younger siblings and getting them through the tragedy. Of course, she'd heard rumblings in town that Travis wasn't at work when he should be, but then the gossips were always going to tell stories, weren't they? "When the baby gets here, we'll all be busy."

Celeste's eyes finally lit up with her customary glimmer. "So true. I wonder if he'll look like Jacob."

"Could be a girl," Marisol said gently.

"No." Celeste shook her head. "This is such a miracle that the baby will be a mini-Jacob. I just know it." She caught herself and gave a slight grin. "But I'd love a girl, too. Don't worry."

Marisol reached for a cloth to wipe a smudge off the counter. "A baby girl would be tons of fun. Just think of the pink blankets, dresses, and shoes."

The bell above the door jangled, and Marylee Rush clipped no-nonsense heels across the checkered floor.

Celeste winked at Marisol and headed for the exit. "Have a nice night." The door closed behind her.

Marisol nodded and automatically stood at attention as Marylee approached the counter. As Senator Rush's mother, Marylee was very active in the community and with her family, ruling with somewhat of an iron fist. "Mrs. Rush. Good evening," Marisol said. "What can I do for you?"

Marylee smoothed down a designer knit suit and pushed back perfectly coiffed gray hair. "I just wanted to double check the order for your Founders' Day booth. We don't want to run out of your special chocolate chip cookies."

Like she'd ever run out. Marisol leaned down for the paperwork. "I think the order is complete, and I'll make sure to add a few extras just in case." Curiosity filled her. They'd gone over this several times already.

Marylee nodded. "Good. It's lovely of you to give back in such a nice way. See how things work out when we help each other?"

Actually, her budget would take quite the hit from donating so many baked goods, but Marisol nodded. "I do see, and of course, you know how much I appreciate the assistance of your family in starting this business." She'd borrowed money from the Rush family when her folks had died, and for some reason, Marylee liked to remind her of that fact every so often. But she really was grateful.

"We have to take care of each other." Marylee bent down to look at the display of cupcakes and cookies. "How is Ginny doing?"

Marisol lifted her head. "She's doing as well as can be expected. It's nice of you to ask."

Marylee straightened and smiled, all polish. "I've been thinking of her. She and my granddaughter are such good friends. That Brittany would never abandon a friend in need."

Marisol hummed in agreement, her mind spinning.

"You know, I've heard Ginny has taken up with Logan Murphy." Marylee gave up the pretense of perusing the desserts.

Where in the world was the conversation going? "Yes. I believe they're becoming very close."

Marylee sniffed. "We truly must be cautious with our young people. Logan is a hero, and I've always so liked the Murphy family."

"They're good people," Marisol agreed, waiting patiently.

"Yes, unlike the Alvarez family. Such a sad story."

Ah ha. Marisol helped her get to the point. "How is your granddaughter doing?"

A sharp gleam entered Marylee's eyes. "How kind of you to ask. In fact, I was hoping you'd have some information about Brittany. I believe that Marcus Alvarez hoodlum is back in town and he's bothering her."

Marisol swallowed. Marcus was a good kid, and she'd been happy to hear he was home to help out his mom. "I haven't heard anything about Marcus and Brittany, but Ginny has been so busy with the baby that we haven't chatted much lately."

Was Brittany dating Marcus Alvarez? That would make the blue-blooded Marylee Rush have a stroke. "I have to tell you, I've always thought Marcus was a good kid in a bad situation. Maybe they're just friends?"

Mrs. Rush lowered her pointy chin. "Brittany has a bright future, and somebody like Marcus will just hold her back. Surely you understand."

Not at all. The bell jangled again, and relief flowed through Marisol until she saw who it was. "Patrick," she murmured.

He still wore the faded jeans that hugged muscled thighs and a dark T-shirt that emphasized his broad chest. So much maleness in one package. His pale blue eyes scrutinized the bakery before landing back on the ladies. "Evening, Mrs. Rush."

Marylee nodded and turned for the door. "Hello, Patrick. Is Murphy's Pub all ready for Founders' Day? I believe you're manning the beer garden at the end of the square?"

"Yes, ma'am. My dad has the schedule all set, and we're ready to work." He held open the door for the older woman. "Is the senator ready with his speech?"

"Of course." Marylee turned at the doorway. "Marisol, please keep me informed if you hear anything about the situation we discussed." Without waiting for an answer, she swept outside.

Patrick let the door shut. "What situation?" He crossed his arms.

Marisol rolled her eyes. "Don't ask." Her hands felt empty, so she grabbed another rag and started wiping down the clean counter.

"Marisol." His voice, low and direct, rumbled all around her.

She breathed in and stood, her nerves jangling. "Patrick, I—"

"No." He held up a hand. "It's time."

Her stomach turned over. Her knees trembled with the need to run, but instead, she lifted her head. If he had something he needed to say, she wouldn't hold him back. "All right."

He cleared his throat and strode toward her, bringing the scent of earth and male with him as he rounded the display case. "We make a good pair."

She nodded and fought the insane urge to tell him that only employees were allowed behind the counter. Hysteria bubbled through her, and she stamped down on the emotion in order to focus. "I like you, Patrick."

He sighed, his powerful shoulders lifting with the movement. "I like you, too. But—"

She'd never know what came over her, but she had to stop those words from coming. Dodging forward, she plastered against him, stretched up on her toes, and kissed him. Not soft, not sweet, but with a desperation she couldn't mask.

He hesitated for about two seconds and then slid one arm around her waist, pulling her up even more. A low groan rumbled up from his chest and rolled into her mouth, sending desire spiraling though her.

He took over the kiss, his mouth firm and sure, strong and masculine. Her thoughts finally blanked until she could do nothing but feel. His hand gripped her ass and squeezed. She gasped into his kiss, her knees wobbling.

The kiss deepened, and he caressed up her butt and underneath her blouse, his warm fingers brushing along her flanks and around her rib cage. Sparks sprang up on her skin, and her abdomen clenched as he trailed his fingers up her torso.

Her breath caught, but she couldn't pull away. His warm hand cupped her breast, and sensation lit her on fire. She moaned.

The bell over the door jangled, and she jumped away.

"Oh my," Celeste said, her cheeks flushing the same pink as the bakery box still in her hands. Her mouth gaped open.

Marisol gulped in air and straightened her shirt, heat flushing up her neck. "I, ah, we—" she croaked.

Patrick moved to the side and discreetly adjusted his jeans.

Oh God. Marisol shook her head. "Celeste—"

Judgment, for the quickest of seconds, flashed across Celeste's face. She banished all expression and forced a smile. "I just, ah, thought I should grab some cookies for Travis. But I'll get them tomorrow." She turned on her heel.

"No, wait," Marisol said, reaching to open the glass case.

"No. Really." Celeste kept going outside into the early evening, and the door shut quietly behind her, her embarrassment remaining in her wake.

Marisol's cheeks burned. She'd seen the fast judgment. Here she was making out in public with Patrick Murphy, her younger sister was pregnant out of wedlock, and her younger brother was out of control and drinking alcohol. As a guardian, she sucked, and no wonder. Her mind wasn't on her duties.

Patrick cleared his throat, and a dimple flickered in his left cheek. "We should probably lock the door next time."

Marisol half-turned, all words clogging in her throat. "What she must be thinking."

Patrick shrugged, his gaze intense. "Who cares what she thinks? It doesn't matter what anybody else thinks."

But it did. Marisol shook her head. "Patrick."

"No." He leaned back against the wall and crossed his arms. "There's no going back, Mari."

She blinked, trying frantically to control the situation. "I just need time."

"No." Regret twisted his lip. "No time. Here's the deal. Either you and I move forward, or we stop."

Anger flashed through her. "You're giving me an ultimatum?"

He grimaced. "Yes. Believe me, I don't want to, but I can't keep standing still like this. We've been dancing around the idea of us for way too long, and it's starting to be painful. I want more."

So did she, but right now, how could she figure out how to give more? At the end of the day, there wasn't anything left. And she'd just been caught making out like an irresponsible teenager by Celeste Salt, who was a superior mother to Ginny by far. "Patrick—"

He held up a hand. "No. Think it over tonight and give me an answer tomorrow. But it's either yes or no—nothing in between. I'm tired of the friend zone, Marisol, and I'm getting out of it. If you let me, I'll be there for you in every way, and we can see what we can build together. If not, then I have to move on."

As an ultimatum, it was a good one. She wanted to hold on to the anger, but it slid from her and left her cold. The man had a point, and she could understand his position. "Tomorrow is kind of soon." It was lame, but she wanted more time to think.

"We've been in limbo for a year," he returned evenly.

She studied him. So tall and strong…why couldn't they just continue as they were? She smoothed back her ruffled hair and then gently touched her still tingling lips. That's why. Even though she wanted to be his friend, she'd almost just had sex with him on the floor of her own shop. If they kept going as is, they'd wind up naked and end their friendship anyway.

He wasn't asking for marriage, which she wasn't ready for. But any relationship with Patrick would have a physical component, and how could she have sex with him while also being a good example for Ginny and Luis? Especially Luis?

"Mari?" Patrick asked.

She sighed and then nodded. "All right. I'll think about it carefully tonight, and I'll let you know my answer tomorrow." Her gut hurt bad enough she already suspected her answer, but there had to be a way to work it out. She couldn't lose Patrick now.

He reached out and ran a knuckle across her cheekbone.

She wanted to lean into his touch, but instead, she moved away.

He leaned over and kissed her forehead before turning and crossing beyond the tables and opening the door. "I'll see you tomorrow, Mari."

She watched him leave, her throat clogging. What was she going to do?

CHAPTER 8

Luis finished wolfing down the last of a cheeseburger right as Marisol pushed open the front door and moved into the living room. He dropped his feet from the scratched coffee table and sat up on the old sofa, reaching for the remote to mute ESPN.

She handed him a box of his favorite—chocolate chip.

The tips of his ears heated. "Thanks."

She slid past him and put a stack of papers on the dinged kitchen table before turning around and crossing her arms. Her dark hair was pulled back, and lines fanned out from her eyes. Worry lines? "We need to talk."

Ah, geez. He cleared his throat. "I'm sorry I got drunk last night." He'd puked all night, and he'd thought his head was going to explode in the morning. After eating bacon and eggs around noon, he'd felt a lot better, and now he was fine but tired. "It won't happen again."

She blinked and suddenly looked so tired he felt even worse. "What were you thinking?" Her tone lacked heat.

He shrugged. "I wasn't thinking. I mean, Mallory was mad at me and stormed off, so I just thought—"

"That you'd drink moonshine?" Marisol hissed.

Ah. There was the anger. Somehow, it was easier to deal with than her disappointment. "Yeah, and it was stupid." He wanted to play sports, and he wanted to get a scholarship, and getting caught drinking would destroy that dream. "Believe me, I know I was lucky Patrick was the one who found me." If it had been the sheriff, he'd probably be in jail.

Marisol shook her head. "You tried to drive. After Ginny's accident, after Jacob died, how could you get behind the wheel?"

The words worked like a sledgehammer to the gut, and he almost bent over. "I'm sorry." It was all he had to give her along with a promise. "I will never drink and drive again. Ever."

She studied him for several moments and then finally sighed. "Is that a bruise under your eye?"

He rubbed his cheekbone. "Lacey punched me when I yelled that I loved Mallory."

Marisol opened her mouth and then shut it again. Finally, she shook her head. "All right. Well, you're grounded for drinking and driving."

He jumped up. "Come on, Marisol. You can't ground me."

She put her hands on her hips. "I'm your legal guardian, and I can ground you. So deal with it."

He shook his head. "But you're my sister."

"Yeah, well, if I had grounded Ginny more, maybe she wouldn't be pregnant, living somewhere else, and dating a guy she barely knows," Marisol ground out.

Luis blinked. "Ginny is fine."

"Ginny is not fine," Marisol said, her eyes filling.

Ah, shoot. Luis moved forward and gave her a hug. His sister was tall, but suddenly he had to bend over to hug her. "Sure she is, and so am I. Stop worrying so much."

Marisol hugged him back and then leaned away. "Stop giving me stuff to worry about."

He grinned. "Okay." Her smile eased the tightness that had been in his chest all day. "I really am sorry."

"I know." She kicked off her shoes and pushed them under the table with her foot.

His yawn almost cracked his jaw. "Do you need me to do anything?"

She lifted an eyebrow. "Like what?"

"I don't know. Anything."

She shook her head. "No, but thanks. I'm going to go through the orders for Founders' Day, and then I'm getting some sleep."

His eyes grew heavy. Being hungover sucked. "Okay, then I'll hit the hay. I have to work tomorrow." He moved through the small house to his room at the back, determined to stop being such a shit to the women in his life. He could do better, and he would.

A navy blue comforter hung off his unmade bed, and clothes littered the floor. A dented wooden desk sat under the window covered with papers and a few socks. His dresser was across the room with stuff scattered across the top. He should probably clean his room at some point.

Instead, he yanked off his shirt and shorts before falling onto the bed. Somehow, he had to stop being such a moron and give Marisol a break. His sister looked like she was dancing on the edge and ready to fall over.

Maybe he should give Ginny a call in the morning and tell her to be nicer to Marisol. It was time for Ginny to grow up, considering she was going to be a mom soon.

Thunder rattled outside, and rain began to pelt down, offering a soothing rhythm that helped him drop into dreamland. He dreamed about puppies and playing at the beach until something jerked him awake in the middle of the night.

His eyelids flipped open, and his heart kicked into gear.

The rain continued outside, and only the red glow from his bedside alarm clock lit the room.

A knock echoed on his window. What the hell? He threw off the bedspread and slowly approached the window, shoving the cheap blinds to the side. "Mallory?" he whispered.

The girl stood in the rain, her hair matted to her head, her hand raised to the glass.

He lifted the blinds and then the window, which had lost its screen years ago. "What are you doing?" he whispered.

She held both hands out to him. "You came to my window the other day, so I figured this was fair game. I wanted to talk."

He naturally took her wet hands and helped ease her onto his desk and into the room. Water dropped from her clothes onto the papers. "About what?" he asked, suddenly aware he was standing there only wearing briefs.

"Us." Her flip-flops hit the floor, and she scooted across the desk to stand.

"Um, okay." His body clamored awake, and he turned to shut the window and blinds before reaching for shorts on the shag carpet. They were kind of clean.

She stilled him with a hand on his wrist. "It about killed me when I saw you with Lacey at the fire. With her hand on your arm."

Luis nodded. "I know, and I'm sorry. Nothing in me wants Lacey, and I really mean that. I love you, and I'm gonna make all of this up to you if it's the last thing I ever do."

Her brown eyes softened, making her look like an angel. "I want to be more than friends."

"Me too." The words burst from him, and he gathered her in a hug. She was so small, and he loved the way they fit. His chest all but exploded, and he leaned back. "I'm sorry about everything. I promise I'll make it up to you. Everything will be okay." He couldn't stop talking.

She smiled and wiped rain off her face. "I know." In her short shorts and tank top, she was his very idea of perfection. "Do you still have the condoms?"

His groin tightened. He swallowed and stepped back, his hands naturally hanging in front of him. "Um, no. My sister took them."

Mallory blushed a pretty pink and reached into her back pocket. "I brought two."

His brain fuzzed. He opened his mouth to say something, but nothing came out.

"Is that enough?" she asked, her gaze on his bare chest.

He had to take several deep breaths before he could talk. "I thought we decided to wait." The bed was right there. The bed was right *there*. Man, she was next to his bed. His body flushed and felt like it was on fire. "Waiting. Remember?"

She shuffled her bare feet on the thick carpet. "I know, but I don't think we should wait. I mean, we're together, right? I want to be all the way together."

All the way.

He shook his head like a dog with a face full of water. "Mallory—"

She moved in and flattened her hands over his abs. "Do you love me?"

Her touch nearly sent him over. "Yes." He did. Everything he had inside him loved her, and he'd almost lost her. If they slept together, could he keep her? "You know I do."

"I love you, too." She slid her hand up and over his chest. Then she stood on her toes and pressed her mouth against his.

He kissed her, using his tongue, shoving all doubts away. They loved each other. She tugged him back and fell onto the bed. He landed on her, and she giggled.

"Shh." He levered up on his elbows so he wouldn't squish her. "We don't want to wake up my sister."

Mallory nodded.

Okay. This was happening. He grabbed the bottom of her tank top and slowly lifted it over her head, leaning back to maneuver. Her bra was white with pretty flowers. "Are you sure about this?"

"Yes." Her eyes wide, she reached down and pushed his briefs down his legs, using her feet when they got to his knees.

Uncertainty stopped him. He was naked with a girl. Okay. He could do this.

She shrugged out of the bra, doing some weird shimmy.

Her breasts sprang free—small and perfect. His body flushed again, and he tried to control himself.

Her hand kind of shook, but she put the condom to her mouth and bit into the foil, spitting it out. "Um, move over a little," she said.

He moved to the side, and she reached down to roll the condom over him. Her hand was soft, and her grip a little too tight. His breath caught, and fire exploded in his stomach. He had to slow her down. "Wait—"

She squeezed the condom into place, and he detonated with a low groan. Shit. His entire body jerked with the force of his orgasm. His eyes closed, and his breath panted out. "God, I'm so sorry."

She gave a small giggle. "Luis."

A pit settled in his stomach. Even though he didn't want to, he opened his eyes to look down at her.

She grinned. "Well, I'm still a virgin. But are you?"

He snorted. Man, he loved her. He wanted to die of embarrassment, and she made it all okay with one little joke.

A banging sounded from outside his bedroom. He jumped off Mallory and grabbed the shorts to pull on, even over the condom.

Mallory slid from the bed and yanked on his sweatshirt, her hair going everywhere. "What is that?"

His lungs seized, and he opened the bedroom door.

The banging was getting louder and coming from the front door. "Mallory Alvarez? Get the hell out here."

She gasped, both hands going to her mouth. "Oh my God. It's my brother."

Luis swayed. "Marcus? How does he know you're here?"

She shook her head. "I don't know." Slipping on her sandals, she moved toward the window.

"Luis?" Marisol called from the hallway, walking closer while tying her white robe.

The pounding got louder.

Marisol caught sight of Mallory. "Mal?" Marisol's eyes widened. "Luis?"

The front door rattled.

"Damn it." Marisol turned on her heel and marched through the house.

Luis leaped into action and reached her side. "Let me answer it."

"No." Marisol pushed him to the side and opened the door. "Stop pounding."

Marcus Alvarez stood in the doorway, fury across his broad face, his hands clenched. "Mallory?" he yelled.

"Geez." Mallory moved out from behind Luis. "Calm down, would you?"

Marcus's dark gaze swept the too-big sweatshirt covering her. "Get out to the car."

"No." She lifted her head.

Marisol looked from brother to sister, shock in her eyes. She cleared her throat. "Marcus? Would you like to come in and sit down?"

"No." Marcus stepped toward his sister. "I'm about to kill somebody, Mallory. Get in the car."

Luis frowned. "Stop scaring her."

Marcus swung his gaze to Luis, and Luis held his ground, even though his gut was churning. Hadn't Marcus spent time in jail?

Marisol tightened her belt, her hands trembling while her voice remained strong. "Everyone calm down. Mallory, what are you doing here?"

"Leave her alone," Luis said before Mallory could answer. "We were just talking and lost track of time."

"Bullshit." Marcus shook his head. "Mom said you snuck out, Mal. I knew just where to find you." His anger sucked the oxygen out of the small living room. "Isn't it enough that you have one knocked-up person in your family already?" he spat out.

Red hazed over Luis's vision, and he moved forward.

"Stop." His sister halted him with one hand on his arm. "Mallory, you should go home with your brother, and we can speak rationally about this in the light of day."

Mallory pushed by Luis, and the empty condom wrapper fell to the ground. The entire room roared into silence, and everybody stared at the package resting on the shag carpet. It must've gotten caught on her shorts.

Marcus bellowed and leaped for Luis, tackling him into the couch. Luis punched out, and Marcus's head jerked back.

"Stop it!" Marisol yelled, grabbing Marcus's hair and yanking him away from Luis.

Marcus didn't fight Marisol and instead let her push him out of the way.

Luis slowly stood, his head ringing, his stomach lurching.

Marisol pushed Marcus toward the door and held out a hand to keep Luis in place. "We're about to become candidates for Jerry Springer, gang." Her voice trembled this time, and in her ratty robe wearing no makeup, she looked like a teenager. "Everyone please stop it."

Mallory moved toward her brother. "Nothing happened, Marcus." She faced Marisol, tears in her eyes. "I promise. Nothing happened."

Luis wanted to reach for her, but Marcus's glare stopped him short.

"Let's go," Marcus said, gesturing his sister toward the storm. "We'll get the car tomorrow."

Mallory left without looking back, and the door shut with a sharp snap.

Luis turned toward his sister.

"What in the world?" she asked, her lip trembling.

He shook his head. "Nothing happened. I promise." Yet a whole lot had happened. Had he just lost Mallory again?

CHAPTER 9

Humidity choked the morning in a way it hadn't in over a year, adding a heaviness to the very air around them. Patrick leaned over and hammered in the post for the beer garden. They worked in the corner of the large park, nearest the pub, and would bring kegs over the morning of the Founders' Day picnic. A small breeze blew through town, and he hoped the weather improved by the day of the event. "When will Tate and Tucker be bringing the hay bales for people to sit on?" His cousins owned a ranch, and they had plenty of hay every year.

Logan shrugged and shoved a large yard umbrella into one of the heavy metal stands to begin forming a shady area. "A day or so before it starts, I think."

Patrick nodded . The sounds of hammering and electric screwdrivers took over the day as the booths went up around the grassy area. The gazebo was ready to go for performers and speech givers, except for the final decorations that would be put up the morning of the events. "Where's Ginny?"

"She dropped by to filch a couple of cupcakes from Marisol."

Just the woman's name slammed Patrick in the gut, and he pushed all thoughts of Marisol out of his head. "How are things with you two, anyway?"

Logan reached for another umbrella; this one had a series of sparkling beer bottles across the top. "We're good." He pushed the post into place, blue eyes somber. "We both have family, but we're alone when we're not together." His shrug spoke volumes and didn't fool his older brother. "It sounds weird, I know."

Yeah, it did sound weird, but Patrick wanted his brother to find peace. "What about the baby?"

Logan scratched his chin. "The baby needs a father."

Patrick jolted. The idea of his younger brother as a father swept concern through him. It was so real. "Are you ready for that? I mean, to take care of Ginny and her baby?"

"I think so." Logan rolled his neck, tension visible in the muscle tightening in his jaw. "I mean, we have a few months to figure that out, you know?"

"Yeah, but I don't think you just date a pregnant woman. Aren't you pretty much all out or all in?" Patrick wiped grime off his forehead.

"Then I'm all in." Logan kicked the umbrella stand farther into the corner. "She needs somebody, and I need her. For some reason, when we're together, all the stress goes away. It's like she understands everything I've gone through, and she brings peace."

Man, the kid had it bad. But maybe, after everything Logan had experienced in the military, he wasn't a kid any longer. "This is a lot," Patrick said.

"I know, but I can protect her. That girl needs cover, and I'm able to provide that. In fact, the idea of keeping her safe eases something in my chest. She's a good person, a fragile one, and she needs me."

"I get that." Hell, Patrick totally understood. "Are you sure she's told you the truth about everything? There are rumors she and Jacob weren't really together that long."

"Fuck rumors." Logan lifted the umbrella, stand and all, to plant in the opposite corner. "She's an honest person, and she'd never lie to me. Our relationship is built on trust and healing."

Patrick nodded. "That's a good foundation. All right, I'll stop questioning you. Whatever you do, I've got your back."

Logan grinned. "Ditto."

Ginny walked around the corner, cupcake box in hand. She had on cute shorts, a flowy blouse, and light sandals.

Logan immediately hustled over and took the box. "How are you feeling?"

"Fine," she said, eyeing Patrick. "Um, hi."

He gave her a gentle smile. The girl probably still wondered what Logan's family thought about him dating a pregnant woman, so he needed to ease her concerns. "Thanks for the cupcakes."

Relief filled her eyes, and her body seemed to relax. "No problem.

My sister didn't mind giving them to us." Ginny chuckled. "I mean, after she grilled me about health and all that stuff."

"Sounds like she cares," Logan said softly.

Ginny nodded. "Yeah, she cares a lot."

Patrick reached for a white cupcake with blue frosting, wanting to ask if Marisol had mentioned him. But considering he wasn't in junior high waiting to be passed a note in study hall, he bit back any questions. He'd have Marisol's answer soon enough.

Dillon headed their way from over by the gazebo, his gun at his belt along with his badge.

Ginny reached for Logan's hand. "I'm thirsty. Want to go get sodas?"

Logan glanced around at the work to be done.

Patrick nodded toward the opposite street. "Dillon can help me. You guys go relax and have a drink. There will be plenty to do later."

Ginny shot him a grateful smile and all but dragged Logan toward the street and restaurants.

Dillon arrived, his gaze on the departing duo. "I wanted to talk to Logan about the hay bales."

"Tucker and Tate are all set to bring them during the final setup." Patrick reached for a couple of nails.

"Ginny takes off whenever she sees me," Dillon mused, rubbing his whiskered chin.

Patrick grinned. "You're the sheriff. She's a young, knocked-up, lonely kid who's dating your youngest brother. Who isn't the father of her baby. Of course she takes off."

Dillon's eyebrows drew down. "Hmm. Good point."

"If they're going to keep dating, you need to somehow make her feel comfortable with you." Patrick hammered a side rail to a post, creating a pseudo-fence.

"How am I supposed to do that?"

Patrick paused and tossed the hammer to catch in his other hand. "I don't know. I guess when the baby is born, buy him a nice present?" He shouldn't be giving anybody advice.

Feminine chatter echoed just before Dakota and Mallory Alvarez rounded the corner of the courthouse and headed their way, stacks of flyers in their hands. Mallory wore faded shorts and a pink T-shirt, while Dakota had on a peach-colored skirt with a fluffy blouse.

The girls reached the beer garden, and Dakota handed him a couple of flyers. "We're supposed to put flyers all over town announcing that the senator will give a speech during Founders' Day."

Mallory rolled her eyes. "Everybody already knows that but we have to deliver all of these."

Patrick took a few flyers. "I'll stick these to a couple of posts and then take a few to the pub later today. Don't worry about going by there."

Dakota smiled and tugged down the rather modest skirt. "Thanks."

"You look nice today, Dakota," Patrick said. The young woman was usually revealing either leg or cleavage, and it was nice to see her respecting herself a little. "Peach is your color."

Dillon cut him a sharp look over the girls' heads.

Dakota blushed, and her eyes brightened. "Thanks. I borrowed the skirt from my mom." She cleared her throat and partially turned to put Dillon in her view. "I'm sorry about the other night in the pub. It's just that I keep thinking my dad will show up at some time."

Dillon's jaw tightened. "It's no problem."

Right. Considering Dillon had run Dakota's dad out of town for good. Well, probably for good. Guys like Hector Alvarez—wife beating, booze swilling assholes—always seemed to turn up again. Patrick folded the flyers and stuck them in his back pocket. "If he shows up at the pub at any time, we'll make sure to call you. Okay?"

She smiled again, her gaze on him. "Thanks, Patrick. You're the best."

Mallory tugged on her older sister's arm. "Let's go and get rid of these things." She turned on a ragged sandal, and her sister followed her, only looking back once before continuing on.

"*You're the best*," Dillon mimicked, tucking his thumbs in his belt loops once the girls were out of earshot.

"Shut up," Patrick retorted, hammering a flyer to the nearest post with one whack. "I feel sorry for her."

"She's trouble, and you should stay as far away from her as possible. God, Patrick. You can't save everybody."

The hair at the back of Patrick's nape prickled. "Really? Considering you're the one who got rid of her father in order to save her mother, I'd say you should listen to your own advice."

"That's different."

"How?" Patrick waited a beat. "Oh. It's different because you like Joanne Alvarez. As in you want to get her naked."

Dillon sighed, and his smart-ass expression dropped. "Okay, maybe I do like her a little, but I'm thinking it'll never happen. On the off chance it does happen, it'd be nice if my brother wasn't dating her daughter, you know? Talk about a mess."

"I have no interest in Dakota Alvarez other than to be nice to her, which not enough people in this world have tried to be with that girl." Patrick grinned. "She could be your stepdaughter if you and Joanne ever give it a shot." The horror crossing Dillon's face made Patrick laugh out loud. "She's not that bad."

"If you say so." Dillon half-turned to see the gazebo, and Patrick followed his gaze. Soon, Senator Rush would be up there, reminding all the citizens why they should vote for him again.

Patrick shook his head.

Running for office would definitely suck, and Patrick couldn't imagine anybody wanting power that much. He was a guy who enjoyed privacy and being able to get the morning paper just wearing his boxers. "You off duty?"

"No. In fact, I should make the rounds." Dillon turned to go. "Call me if you need anything."

"Sure thing." Patrick reached for another slat to make the fence. He worked by himself for almost an hour, whistling a country tune, his mind on Dillon and his pursuit of Joanne Alvarez. Well, not his pursuit. More like his protecting her from afar.

"Patrick?" A soft voice jerked him from his musings.

He turned from nailing the last of the fence slats into place, his heart thundering. "Marisol. Hi."

Her dark hair curled around her shoulders, and her even darker eyes seemed somber. She was everything feminine and pretty in the world, and he wanted nothing more than to kiss her right then and there. But he remained in place.

"Hi." She smoothed down a flowing skirt with her hands, her gaze darting around before landing back on him. Bluish circles marred the soft skin under her eyes, which looked a little bloodshot.

He sighed. "Did you get any sleep last night?"

"Not really." She wrung her hands together. "Mostly because Marcus Alvarez showed up, pounded on my door, and insisted his sister get her butt out of my house. At three in the morning."

Patrick's eyebrows rose. "Uh, Dakota or Mallory?"

"Mallory." Marisol pushed a wayward curl out of her eyes. "Luis said they didn't have sex, but there was a condom wrapper and Marcus went nuts."

Patrick's head jerked up. "Did he hurt you?"

Marisol frowned. "Of course not. He was just angry, which I can't really blame him."

No, neither could Patrick. "The hay won't be delivered until closer to Founders' Day, so I can't offer you a seat."

"That's okay. I'd rather stand." She shuffled her feet.

Well, that couldn't be good. "Planning to make a fast getaway?" He tried to joke, but his words sounded hollow.

She stared at his chest. "Funny. I thought about it, I really did, Patrick. You're a great guy—"

"Ah, hell." He was a great guy. The kind of guy who belonged in the friend zone forever. "You don't have to—"

"I do." Her pretty eyes finally lifted to meet his gaze. "I just can't do it right now. Ginny's a mess, and I'm afraid she's heading for trouble. Luis is in trouble and is spiraling out of control. I have to be a good example, and I have to concentrate on them."

The words she spoke, all put together like that, seemed so harmless. But they pierced through him like a knife he'd taken to the leg in a fishing accident years ago. Sharp and directed squarely to his chest this time. "I could help you," he said softly.

She shook her head. "No, you couldn't. I owe it to my folks and to them. To be there a hundred percent."

He cleared his throat, his lungs feeling empty. "All right."

"Patrick, I'm so—"

"Don't say it." He held up a hand, trying to keep his temper at bay. "Don't say you're sorry. Please."

"Okay." Tears filled her eyes.

Frustration bubbled though him. "I should get back to work."

She nodded and glanced around, finally turning. "Okay. Bye."

"Bye." He watched her walk away, and not once did she turn back to look.

He'd been kicked by a cousin's horse once—right in the center of the chest. Oh, he'd dodged with just enough time to end up bruised and not broken, but he'd been in pain for nearly a month as he healed up.

This felt worse.

CHAPTER 10

Ginny liked the feeling of her hand in Logan's. His grip remained firm but somehow gentle, and without seeming to, he moved her so she walked on the inside of the sidewalk and he walked by the road. Protecting her.

He moved with the natural grace of a man who could leap into action at any second, and with the watchful eye of a guy who had seen hell and wouldn't be surprised to see it again.

They walked along Second Street and waited for the light to cross onto Pecan. "You know, you're not breaking the law by dating me," Logan said, his gaze sweeping the entire area like usual.

Ginny's gait hitched. "Um, I know."

He glanced down and smiled, his blue eyes sparkling. "Then we don't have to run away every time Dillon comes near."

She opened her mouth to argue and then gave him the truth. "I can't help it. For some reason, the sheriff makes me feel guilty." Maybe it was because she might've lied to the whole town about who had fathered her baby? Well, she had lied about having a long relationship with Jacob, considering they'd only had one night. She struggled to explain to Logan. "I mean, I'm pregnant, and you could have any girl you wanted. I come with baggage."

He chuckled and slid an arm around her shoulder. "A baby is a blessing and isn't baggage. I have baggage, and you're okay with that."

Sure. His baggage came with being a hero, and hers came from being a slut. But she couldn't tell him that. A part of her, a lonely scared part, wanted to tell him that she'd slept with Senator Rush, many times, and that he could be the baby's father. If Logan stayed with her, he'd protect her from Sebastian. But he wouldn't stay with her if he knew the truth, would he? "I think you're amazing," she said.

He tugged her closer into his strong body. "You're amazing, and you need to stop worrying. We're going to be fine."

They reached the door to the Bluebonnet Cafe, and she stopped, turning to face him. "I'm not amazing. I've made so many mistakes. I'm not good like you."

He swooped down and planted a hard kiss on her mouth that shot sparks through her entire body. His knuckle lifted her chin, and his eyes were right above hers when he spoke. "No more of that, Ginny. You're good, you're honest, and we have something real and true here. I've trusted you with my heart, and you've done the same. Got it?"

Her heart trembled against her rib cage. She wasn't good and honest, but she couldn't lose him. She just couldn't. So she smiled, determined to spend the rest of her life making him happy. "I've got it."

His approval warmed parts of her she'd thought would always be frozen. "That's my girl. Now, let's eat." He took her hand again and stepped inside, pausing to scout the room.

She stood quietly behind him, having gotten used to his need to survey any area. Someday he might relax, but for now, his training always kicked in. Finally he gave a quick wave toward a booth in the back. "Marcus and Brittany are here."

Ginny smiled and allowed him to lead her to the back of the restaurant, not even caring if stupid old biddies gossiped about her this time. She was with a great guy who made her happy. Who cared what anybody else in town thought? They didn't know her or what she'd been through, and they didn't know what Logan had been through, but together, she and Logan were strong again.

Logan stood aside so she could scoot into the booth and sit across from her best friend, Brittany Rush. They'd been friends since childhood, and the thought that Ginny had slept with Brittany's dad still made her sick. But she was going to take that secret to the grave and forget about it right this second. Brittany could never know.

"I'm so glad you guys came in," Brittany said, her eyes sparkling.

Ginny smiled back. Brittany was town royalty, and Marcus was rougher than rough from the tough side of the tracks, but together they looked right. If it lasted, her folks were going to freak.

"Have you guys eaten?" Ginny asked.

Brittany shook her head, playing with the handle of her fork. "Nope. Your timing is perfect." She practically beamed as she looked from Ginny to Logan and back. "Just perfect." Marcus laid his hand over hers in a very sweet move.

Ginny warmed. They were both dating their schoolgirl crushes, and life was pretty damn good. Maybe she could actually be happy. She placed her palm over her slightly rounded tummy.

They ate cheeseburgers and fries, carefree for the first time in so long. When the bill came, Marcus grabbed it before anybody else could.

"I'll split it with you," Logan said, reaching for his wallet.

"Nope. This one is on me." Marcus turned dark eyes toward Brittany. "Any objections?"

She grinned. "Not a chance. I learned my lesson the other night."

Marcus smiled, flashing a dimple that had made more than one cheerleader swoon back in high school. "Now, that I like to hear." He counted out bills to place on the table and then pushed from the booth, holding back a hand to assist Brittany. "We have to go, folks."

Brittany took his hand, her brows drawing down. "We do?"

"Yep." He smacked Logan on the shoulder. "I'll catch up with you later."

"Count on it," Logan returned, amusement in his eyes. He waited until the couple had left before turning toward Ginny. "What do you think about them?"

Ginny looked out the window to watch her best friend and Marcus walk down Pecan Street. "I think if they care about each other, they have a good shot." She turned back to stare into the sexiest blue eyes she'd ever seen. "What do you think?"

"I couldn't agree more." He glanced out the window and frowned. "There are Dakota and Mallory. I wonder what they're up to?"

Ginny turned to see the sisters across the street, flyers in their hands. "They're on the promotional committee for Founders' Day. It's too bad Marcus missed them." He would probably have liked seeing his sisters working together, even if they didn't seem to be talking while they walked.

"Marcus seemed to have other things on his mind," Logan said, a smile in his voice.

Ginny nodded and turned back. She slid her hand beneath Logan's as if she had every right to do so. "Yeah. Brittany."

"I have something on my mind, too."

Ginny pressed her lips together, trying not to smile like an idiot. "You do, huh? What might that be?"

"This." He leaned in, and his lips covered hers in a promise she couldn't help but accept. Life began now, and with him. Nothing would ruin what they had.

* * * *

Brittany Rush tried to walk like a dignified adult and not skip like a happy kid while holding Marcus Alvarez's hand in public. At first, he'd been all weird about them dating, but he seemed to have jumped in with a vengeance.

Maybe with too much enthusiasm? Was it because he was going to leave her and go back to Montana? Man, she hoped he changed his mind about that.

They passed the edge of the Bluebonnet Cafe and kept walking next to an empty lot that had been concreted years ago as extra parking. During the festival the lot would be crammed full, but today only a lone Ford Fiesta rested at the far end near the Sports Shack.

A breeze filtered through the humid day, and she pushed hair out of her face. "Um, I really like you, Marcus." Her voice came out tentative.

He paused, halting her alongside him. "Okay." His brows furrowed over a face just too handsome to be real. "What's going on, Brit?"

She liked that he called her Brit. Her family insisted on her full name being used by the press and by anybody talking about her, and the nickname from Marcus sent tingles through her abdomen. She didn't know how to be coy, so she went for the truth. "I know my grandmother saw us kissing in the park the other day, and I know you saw her, too." Grams had insulted Marcus the first chance she got, and surely that had made Marcus mad and hurt his feelings.

Marcus lifted his chin. "Yeah, so?"

Man, she wished she had more experience with men. "So? I just want to make sure that this is about you and me, and not you being pissed at her."

For a second, thunderclouds seemed to fill Marcus's eyes. He studied her, almost seeing through her it felt, and then his expression softened. "That's fair."

She blinked and tried to take a step back, but he held her in place.

"Um—"

"Your grandmother is a judgmental bully, and she did make me mad." Marcus pulled Brittany closer and settled his hands on her hips. "But this is all about you and me. I like you." He slid a hand up and tangled it in her hair, tilting back her head. "You're smart, sweet, and so beautiful it hurts." Then he slanted his mouth over hers and kissed her deep.

Her knees actually wobbled. She returned the kiss, caught up in the storm unleashed by a man wilder than she could ever hope. Would he stay in Texas?

Finally, he released her.

Her lips tingled, and her body craved. Oh, she'd kissed boys before, but they didn't come close to Marcus. He was all man. She was close enough she could feel how hard he'd become in his jeans.

He glanced down at her lips, and his nostrils flared.

She lifted her chin. "I don't know where we're going, but I really like you, too."

They had issues, there was no doubt. Her family would be a problem, but this was a good man, and she wanted to be with him. To see what they could create together. She'd never felt like this before, and giving him up would hurt too much. She wouldn't pressure him. She'd just prove to him that he should stay with her and not return to Montana. "I'm having fun with you."

His smile was strong and sweet—and nearly as potent as his kiss. "Good. I brought you a present." Taking something from his back pocket, he placed a box in her hands.

She read the box, and her heart just swelled. "Marcus." Tears actually pricked the back of her eyes.

"Hey." He rubbed her cheekbone. "These were supposed to make you happy."

"They do." She looked up at him through blurry eyes and then back down at the box of colored chalk. "I can't believe you bought these." She'd mentioned just once that she wished she would've had the kind of parents to get on the ground and draw with chalk, and look what he'd done.

"Good." He opened the box and handed her a blue piece of chalk, while he took an orange one.

Most girls would've wanted diamonds or gold, but the simple box of chalk stole her heart and made it his. "Thank you."

"You're welcome." Turning her around, he gave her a gentle push toward the empty lot. "We have a lot of ground to cover. Let's start coloring, baby."

CHAPTER 11

Dakota Alvarez sighed and tacked yet another flyer to a bulletin board. She was sore from her time with the senator a couple of nights ago at the cabin, and that made her uneasy. He'd never treated her like that before.

When she'd gone over to Marisol's for movie night right after Marcus had finally returned home, she and Mallory had pretty much ignored each other. But they'd been assigned to post flyers together, and since Dakota was trying to be more dignified, she could take the high road with her little sister. "I'm, ah, sorry I said those things about Luis. I heard he didn't really sleep with Lacey."

Mallory flushed red and nodded, hurrying out the door of the Five & Dime. "I know, and don't worry. Lacey tried her best, but he turned her down."

"I'm sorry I yelled at you, and I'm really sorry I hit you." The idea that she'd slapped her sister still made Dakota want to throw up. "It was wrong, and I was just so mad about Dad leaving."

"I know." Mallory sighed. "We're not going to agree about him, ever, but maybe we can just not talk about him to each other."

They didn't really have a choice, it seemed. "Okay." The wind slapped into Dakota, and she pushed a tendril of hair out of her face. She'd put it up in a fancy knot at the base of her neck like the ladies did in the fashion magazines. Her sandals clipped on the pavement, and for once her feet didn't hurt since the heels were so small.

"Luis is a good guy, and Lacey was trying to break us up," Mallory said, her lips tightening. "She's gone off the deep end."

Her little sister needed to learn to fight dirty. "You need to make sure

Lacey stays away from your man. I mean, if you want Luis to be your man," Dakota said. He was a cute kid with nice muscles, but he probably wasn't going anywhere in life.

"I love him," Mallory said, pausing in front of the hair salon. "He loves me, too."

Dakota lifted an eyebrow and paused. "Then you need to secure that and soon."

Mallory leaned back against the window. "Secure it?"

"Yeah." Dakota moved closer to her sister. "Guys are led around by their dicks, and if you want him to stay yours, you're gonna have to give it up."

Mallory rolled her eyes, and her blush deepened. "Geez, Dakota. It's possible for a guy to stay with you without sex."

God, she was so stupid. "Maybe if Mom had had sex with dad once in a while, he wouldn't have left her." Anger at the unfairness of it all roared through her.

Mallory winced. "Eww. They probably had sex—and we're not talking about him, remember?"

Ha. Their mother couldn't do anything right, and that was probably another place the woman had failed. "You're right. No more talking about either of them. Why don't you go put some flyers in the salon?"

Mallory sighed and stomped inside to the reception desk, where she left several flyers. She walked out just as Ginny Moreno and Logan Murphy strolled by on the other side of the street. Mallory waved to Ginny, who waved back and kept on walking toward the park and the Storm Oak, which was down the way.

Dakota shook her head, her fury expanding. That bitch had stolen Jacob Salt from her, and they would've had a wonderful life. He certainly wouldn't have been in a car driven by Ginny, who obviously couldn't drive in a storm. Hell, she'd killed Jacob, really. And now she was hanging out with the youngest Murphy, who was hot on a hottie stick. "What in the world does Logan see in her? I mean, she's knocked-up with another guy's kid."

Mallory shrugged. "She's nice."

"Right. She's so nice that she's taking advantage of the Salts. Moving in there and expecting Jacob's grieving family to take care of her just because she seduced him and couldn't figure out how to use a condom." Dakota snorted. It was a good plan, damn it.

Mallory moved to cross Second Street. "Well, according to Celeste, the pregnancy is a huge miracle. So she probably wants to help out."

Dakota rolled her eyes and stepped over a puddle to follow her sister. "Whatever." She reached the other side and scraped a little grass off her small heel.

Mallory paused and glanced at her skirt. "Why are you dressed like that, anyway?"

"Like what?" Dakota set her stance and tried to keep her voice level.

Mallory frowned. "Like a lady going to tea in the fifties. I mean, that's Mom's skirt, and those are her shoes, right?"

"Yeah, so? Maybe I just wanted to try something new." Dakota pointed to the few remaining flyers. "Let's get this over with. You get the businesses on Cedar Street, and I'll do the ones on Live Oak after getting some more flyers. We're almost out."

"You are so weird." Mallory turned to head into the Hill Country Savings and Loan.

Dakota fought the urge to call her sister back to make sure she looked okay in the outfit. The other night, bent over the table at the cabin, she'd realized that the senator needed to see her potential as his wife. Dakota had been so busy falling for him and exploring their adult relationship that she hadn't shown that side of herself.

She could be classy.

In fact, if she was going to be with him at all times, she needed to be classy and dignified. So she'd borrowed her mother's boring skirt and shoes, and she'd put her hair up while wearing minimal makeup. Without her tons of mascara and lipstick, she felt naked.

But he liked her naked, now didn't he?

A breeze filtered through her thin blouse and she shivered. She hadn't talked to him since the night at the cabin, and he hadn't texted her. She hunched her shoulders forward and then remembered to straighten her back. Posture was important. Plus, it pushed out her boobs.

So she dug deep for courage and walked past the wide windows of the Savings and Loan, where she unfortunately worked, to reach the front door of Senator Rush's headquarters. Steeling her shoulders, she marched up the nicely bricked stoop and pushed open the glass-front door to an empty reception area fronted by an oak desk.

It was noon, so the place was quiet.

Her hands trembled, so she wiped them down her skirt before

walking behind the counter like she had every right to do so. Several tables covered with election materials were scattered around, with two offices in the back next to a kitchen.

Low voices could be heard from the corner office. She hesitated. It wasn't too late to run back outside. But no, Dakota Alvarez wasn't a coward, and she belonged there, damn it. She hastened around the tables for the senator's office.

He stood over to the side, leaning over his desk and reading a document held by a young office worker in a tight skirt. Brunette with big boobs and blue eyes—maybe about eighteen?

Dakota stood in the doorway, her breath catching.

"I like this design," the girl said.

"Me too." Sebastian patted the girl on the shoulder. The sleeves of his white dress shirt were rolled up to show his strong forearms, and with his black pants, he looked every bit the powerful man he'd become. "It's beautiful, Anna," he said, his tone a low purr.

Fire roared through Dakota until her skin ached. He was standing way too close to the girl, and he was using that voice. The one he normally used with her. "Excuse me." Her voice came out more forcefully than she'd intended.

Both Sebastian and the girl jumped.

Sebastian recovered quicker. "Miss Alvarez?"

As opposed to *my bad girl*—the nickname he'd given her a while ago. She bit her lip to keep from saying it out loud. "Yes, Senator. We're out of the flyers you wanted spread around town, and I thought I'd pick up some more." She spoke through gritted teeth. What would he do if she leaped across the room and scratched out good ole Anna's eyes? That'd show him.

Anna glanced at the senator and back at Dakota, obviously catching undercurrents.

Sebastian stepped away. "I don't know if there are any more flyers. Why don't you come back after lunch when the campaign staff is here?"

Hurt slithered through her, and her ears rang. The man thought he'd blow her off? After what she'd let him do to her the other night that still made her walk funny? "I'd also like to talk to you about the project we discussed the other night at your cabin."

Alarm flashed in his eyes, and then his polite smile lifted his lips. "Of course." He took Anna's elbow and escorted her toward the door. "Anna, why don't you go tweak the top design, and after Miss Alvarez and I figure out how the local youth can create a campaign slogan for first time voters, I'll look at it again?"

Anna nodded and scooted by Dakota, letting out a sigh as she made it past.

Dakota swept inside, her head held high, her knees wobbling.

The senator quietly closed the door. "What the hell are you doing here?" he hissed, keeping his voice down.

She turned and put both hands on her hips. "I figured after the other night, you'd be calling me." With presents. Big-assed presents. "You haven't called."

He stalked around his massive desk to take a seat. A picture of the White House in full sun took up the entire wall behind him. "I've announced my reelection bid, and I'm busy, which you know."

That wasn't all. Even now, he was glancing at his computer and not at her. She stomped her foot. "Stop ignoring me."

He sighed and glanced up. "Dakota, you can't be here. I'm an elected official, and I'm married."

"For now," Dakota snapped back.

His chin lifted, and his eyes hardened. "Meaning what?"

A chill skittered down her back. "Meaning, we could be so good together."

He blinked and sat back in his chair. "I've been honest with you from the start."

Yeah, but he had to see the real her. They needed to get back onto the same track, so she pouted out her lip. "I know, and I'm sorry, but I had to see you."

His gaze warmed and swept down her front. "What are you wearing?"

She lifted a shoulder. "Something different."

"No, Dakota." He shook his head. "That isn't you. I've never asked you to be anybody but you."

Well, that was true. She smiled and suddenly felt so much better. "It seems like you're pulling away." Why not try honesty?

He reached into a drawer, stood, and crossed around the room to stand before her. The expensive scent of his cologne wafted around them. "It's just the campaign, sweetheart. I have to concentrate and get all my ducks in a row." He held out a small box.

She held back a squeal and took the box, flipping the velvet open to reveal a delicate silver necklace with a sapphire pendant. "Oh, Sebastian, it's beautiful," she breathed.

"So are you." He freed the necklace and motioned for her to turn around for him to clasp the beautiful piece around her neck.

"Thank you." She turned and levered up on her toes to place a kiss on his chin.

He smiled and patted her back before returning to his desk and reading his computer. "I'll give you a call," he said absently.

Dakota lost her smile. "Okay." She opened the door and walked right into the senator's mother.

Marylee Rush stepped back. "Oh, my."

"I'm so sorry." Heat climbed into Dakota's face. "I was here, um, looking for more flyers."

Marylee's gaze sharpened, and she glanced at her son and then back at Dakota. "I'm sure the senator is too busy to worry about flyers, dear."

"Um, of course." Dakota ducked her head and brushed by the woman, taking a moment to notice her sensible but designer shoes and handbag.

"Wait a minute." Mrs. Rush's cultured tone stopped her cold. "Why don't I walk you out?"

"Mother?" Sebastian protested. "I could use your help here."

The smile Mrs. Rush flashed was all teeth. "I'm sure you could, Sebastian. I'll be right back." She pivoted and led the way through the tables like a general on the march, skirting the reception desk and clipping right outside.

Nausea dropped into Dakota's stomach, but she followed in the wake of the woman's expensive perfume. The kind of perfume Dakota would someday wear. In fact, next time she was with the senator, she'd mention that she needed perfume.

Yeah. She knew the senator better than his own mother did, now didn't she? With a smile tickling her lips, Dakota followed Mrs. Rush outside onto the brick stoop. "You didn't have to walk me out. I'll be back after lunch for more flyers."

Mrs. Rush rounded on her and leaned in, her eyes a fiery blue. "No. There's absolutely no need for you to return later. My son and his wife appreciate your help with the flyers, but you've done quite enough."

Dakota took a step back. "But I—"

"You nothing." Derision twisted the older woman's mouth. "Your *assistance* is now over. Do you understand me?"

Dakota's mouth gaped open. Suddenly, in her mother's sensible clothes, she felt like a fool.

Her jaw tightened, and her shoulders shot back. Tears clogged in her throat, but she ruthlessly swallowed them down. If she married the senator, she'd have to learn to deal with women like Marylee. Without another word, she turned and sauntered down the steps, making sure her ass swayed just enough.

The woman might think she could control Sebastian as well as Dakota, but she was freakin' crazy. The senator cared about Dakota, probably more than even he knew.

Now all Dakota had to do was prove it to both of them. Whether his mother liked it or not, Dakota Alvarez would be wearing the man's ring within a month.

Damned if she wouldn't.

<<<<>>>>

About Rebecca Zanetti

New York Times Bestselling author Rebecca Zanetti is the author of over twenty-five dark paranormals, romantic suspense, and contemporary romances, and her books have appeared multiple times on the USA Today, NY Times, Amazon, Barnes and Noble, and iBooks bestseller lists. She lives in the wilds of the Pacific Northwest with her own Alpha hero, two kids, a couple of dogs, a crazy cat…and a huge extended family. She believes strongly in luck, karma, and working her butt off…and she thinks one of the best things about being an author, unlike the lawyer she used to be, is that she can let the crazy out. Her current series are: The Scorpius Syndrome, The Dark Protectors, The Realm Enforcers, The Maverick Montana Cowboys, and the Sin Brothers series. Find Rebecca at: www.rebeccazanetti.com

Sign up for the Rising Storm/1001 Dark Nights Newsletter and be entered to win an exclusive lightning bolt necklace specially designed for Rising Storm by Janet Cadsawan of Cadsawan.com.

Go to http://risingstormbooks.com/necklace to subscribe.

As a bonus, all subscribers will receive a free Rising Storm story
Storm Season: Ginny & Jacob – the Prequel
by Dee Davis

Rising Storm

Storm, Texas.

Where passion runs hot, desire runs deep, and secrets have the power to destroy…

Nestled among rolling hills and painted with vibrant wildflowers, the bucolic town of Storm, Texas, seems like nothing short of perfection.

But there are secrets beneath the facade. Dark secrets. Powerful secrets. The kind that can destroy lives and tear families apart. The kind that can cut through a town like a tempest, leaving jealousy and destruction in its wake, along with shattered hopes and broken dreams. All it takes is one little thing to shatter that polish.

Rising Storm is a series conceived by Julie Kenner and Dee Davis to read like an on-going drama. Set in a small Texas town, *Rising Storm* is full of scandal, deceit, romance, passion, and secrets. Lots of secrets.

Look for these Rising Storm books!

Tempest Rising by Julie Kenner
Ginny Moreno didn't mean to do it, but when she came home to Storm, she brought the tempest with her. And now everyone will be caught in its fury...

White Lightning by Lexi Blake
As the citizens of Storm, Texas, sway in the wake of the death of one of their own, Daddy's girl Dakota Alvarez also reels from an unexpected family crisis ... and finds consolation in a most unexpected place.

Crosswinds by Elisabeth Naughton
Lacey Salt's world shattered with the death of her brother, and now the usually sweet-tempered girl is determined to take back some control—even if that means sabotaging her best friend, Mallory, and Mallory's new boyfriend, Luis.

Dance in the Wind by Jennifer Probst
During his time in Afghanistan, Logan Murphy has endured the unthinkable, but reentering civilian life in Storm is harder than he imagined. But when he is reacquainted with Ginny Moreno, a woman who has survived terrors of her own, he feels the first stirrings of hope.

Calm Before the Storm by Larissa Ione
Marcus Alvarez fled Storm when his father's drinking drove him over the edge. With his mother and sisters in crisis, Marcus is forced to return to the town he thought he'd left behind. But it is his attraction to a very grown up Brittany Rush that just might be enough to guarantee that he stays.

Take the Storm by Rebecca Zanetti
Marisol Moreno has spent her youth taking care of her younger siblings. Now, with her sister, Ginny, in crisis, and her brother in the throes of his first real relationship, she doesn't have time for anything else. Especially not the overtures of the incredibly compelling Patrick Murphy.

Weather the Storm by Lisa Mondello, Coming November 5, 2015

Bryce Douglas faces a crisis of faith when his idyllic view of his family is challenged with his son's diagnosis of autism. Instead of accepting his wife and her tight-knit family's comfort, he pushes them away, fears from his past threatening to undo the happiness he's found in his present.

Thunder Rolls by Dee Davis
In the season finale …

As Hannah Grossman grapples with the very real possibility that she is dating one Johnson brother while secretly in love with another, the entire town prepares for Founders Day. The building tempest threatens not just Hannah's relationship with Tucker and Tate, but everyone in Storm as dire revelations threaten to tear the town apart.

… Season 2 coming in 2016. Sign up for the newsletter so you don't miss a thing. http://risingstormbooks.com

And coming this spring, a two episode mini-season before Season two launches in September, 2016!

Weather the Storm
Rising Storm Episode 7
By Lisa Mondello

Secrets, Sex and Scandals …

Welcome to Storm, Texas, where passion runs hot, desire runs deep, and secrets have the power to destroy… Get ready. The storm is coming.

Bryce Douglas faces a crisis of faith when his idyllic view of his family is challenged with his son's diagnosis of autism. Instead of accepting his wife and her tight-knit family's comfort, he pushes them away, fears from his past threatening to undo the happiness he's found in his present.

* * * *

Tara hesitated. "You heard what the doctor said. We've got to start working on a strategy for helping him cope."

Bryce quickly glanced at the calendar on his desk. With so many people using electronics to plan their days, he still preferred the old-fashioned daily planner where he could give it a quick glance and know exactly what he was doing.

Bryce tapped the blotter on his desk. "I have an appointment in the afternoon."

"You'll have to change it."

He glanced up at his wife. Tara had never been a demanding woman. She knew the importance of his job as a pastor. But the expression on her face told him she was serious. And he knew she was right. He should be there. But he wasn't sure he could face it. Tara was stronger. She could handle the meeting. Later, when he'd had more time…

"I have a full schedule tomorrow, Tara. Can't we deal with all of this when the next session starts?"

Her agitation grew right before his eyes. "You're going to have to fit us in your schedule, Bryce."

The tone of Tara's voice startled him. She knew his time was always filled with meetings, prayer for people who'd lost someone or something. His congregation depended on him for counsel and he took that responsibility seriously.

"Tara?"

"Change it. I mean it. You move your schedule around all the time for other people. You miss dinner with your family to go counsel people in crisis. You…I know your position in the church is important. But we're important too. Whoever it is you're seeing tomorrow can rearrange their schedule for you this time."

Guilt washed through him. He loved his wife. But he couldn't do it. He just wasn't ready. "Tara, you of all people should know what a difficult time this is for the people of Storm. Jacob Salt was a fine young man known to this entire community. People in this town are hurting."

"Look around, Bryce. People in this house are hurting too."

She turned and left the office, leaving him staring at a void that she used to fill.

1001 Dark Nights

Welcome to 1001 Dark Nights… a collection of novellas that are breathtakingly sexy and magically romantic. Some are paranormal, some are erotic. Each and every one is compelling and page turning.

Inspired by the exotic tales of The Arabian Nights, 1001 Dark Nights features *New York Times* and *USA Today* bestselling authors.

In the original, Scheherazade desperately attempts to entertain her husband, the King of Persia, with nightly stories so that he will postpone her execution.

In our version, month after month, each of our fabulous authors puts a unique spin on the premise and creates a tale that a new Scheherazade tells long into the dark, dark night.

For more information about 1001 Dark Nights, visit www.1001DarkNights.com.

On behalf of Rising Storm,
Liz Berry, M.J. Rose, Julie Kenner & Dee Davis would like to thank ~

Steve Berry
Doug Scofield
Melissa Rheinlander
Kim Guidroz
Jillian Stein
InkSlinger PR
Asha Hossain
Chris Graham
Pamela Jamison
Kasi Alexander
Jessica Johns
Dylan Stockton
Richard Blake
The Dinner Party Show
and Simon Lipskar

Made in the USA
Charleston, SC
19 January 2016